THE REICH FLIES THE FLAG

Recent Titles by Leo Kessler from Severn House

Writing as Leo Kessler

S.S.*Wotan Series*
Assault On Baghdad
Death's Eagles
The Great Escape
Hitler Youth Attacks!
Kill Patton
Operation Glenn Miller
Operation Iraq
Operation Leningrad
Patton's Wall
The Screaming Eagles
Sirens of Dunkirk
Wotan Missions

Battle for Hitler's Eagles' Nest
The Blackout Murders
The Churchill Papers
Murder at Colditz
The Blackout Murders

Writing as Duncan Harding

Assault on St Nazaire
Attack New York!
Clash in the Baltic
The Finland Mission
Hell on the Rhine
The Normandie Mission
Operation Judgement
Operation Torch
Sink the Ark Royal
Sink the Bismarck
Sink the Cossack
Sink the Graf Spee
Sink HMS Kelly
Sink the Hood
Sink the Prince of Wales
Sink the Scharnhorst
Sink the Tirpitz
Sink the Warspite
Slaughter in Singapore
The Tobruk Rescue

THE REICH FLIES
THE FLAG

Leo Kessler

This first world edition published in Great Britain 2005 by
SEVERN HOUSE PUBLISHERS LTD of
9–15 High Street, Sutton, Surrey SM1 1DF.
This first world edition published in the USA 2006 by
SEVERN HOUSE PUBLISHERS INC of
595 Madison Avenue, New York, N.Y. 10022.

British Library Cataloguing in Publication Data

Kessler, Leo, 1926-
    The Reich flies the flag
    1.   World War, 1939-1945 - Campaigns - Soviet Union - Fiction
    2.   World War, 1939-1945 - Propaganda - Fiction
    3.   Nazi propaganda - Soviet Union - Fiction
    4.   Suspense fiction
    I.   Title
    823.9'14 [F]

    ISBN-10: 0-7278-6300-2

'Wherever the swastika flag flies is German. Not for a day, a month, even a year, but for eternity!'
Adolf Hitler, 1942.

AUTHOR'S NOTE

On the morning of August 23rd, 1942, an urgent signal was received at Hitler's headquarters in East Prussia. It was so important that Hitler's butler Heinz Linge dared to wake the Führer. Under other circumstances, Hitler would have been terribly annoyed to be woken before eleven o'clock; he valued his sleep. Not now. He took off his nightcap, smoothed back his dyed black hair and adjusted his gold-rimmed spectacles – in which it was a punishable offence to photograph him – and read the signal excitedly. After all, he had been waiting for it for days now.

It read.

'Mission accomplished. At exactly fifteen hundred hours on 21 August 1942, my soldiers of the High Alpine Corps planted our holy flag on the west peak of Mount Elbrus
    Dietl, General of Mountain Troops'

Hitler was overjoyed. As he sat on his chamber pot in his simple white cotton nightshirt, he spoke animatedly to the tall butler, who held the rank of colonel in the Waffen SS. 'My God, Linge, what an achievement!'

Indeed it was. Deep behind Russian lines, a small group of bold German mountain soldiers had planted the Nazi swastika flag – the blood-red symbol of National Socialist determination to rule the world – on Russia's highest mountain, only a few thousand feet smaller than Everest itself. In the midst of total war, they had carried out a climbing first that would have been damnably difficult even in peacetime.

But Hitler's boast that Mount Elbrus, like all the other foreign territories which Germany had conquered from the

English Channel to the Russian Ural Mountains, would always remain in Nazi hands came to naught. On February 13th, 1943, a Russian team finally reached the summit of Elbrus and tore down the hated German flag. By then the battles of El Alamein and Stalingrad had been fought and won by the Allies and Germany had lost the war.

L. Kessler, Spring 2005.

PART ONE
Enter Colonel Sturmer

One

' **A** symbol, Bormann.'

Martin Bormann, Hitler's secretary, as crawlingly attentive as ever, rubbed his fleshy hands together, and asked, 'What did you say, *Mein Führer*?'

For a moment or two, Adolf Hitler didn't reply. Instead he listened to the faint sound of the bells coming up from the valley far below and watched the red, green and silver rockets sailing into the night sky, celebrating the New Year. Naturally it was forbidden to break the blackout in this manner, especially in the neighbourhood of the Führer's own home, the Eagle's Nest. But on New Year's Eve, 1941, the Führer had decreed that the blackout regulations should not be observed so strictly.

As he had told Bormann earlier, in the early hours of morning, as his New Year's Eve guests had departed, replete with caviar and champagne, 'Who can attack us now, my dear chap? The English are out of the war virtually and the Reds soon will be. Germany rules Europe from Calais to the Caspian Sea and from Norway to North Africa. We are the masters of 300 million Europeans. Who dare attempt to bomb us? Let the peasants have their fun. They have worked hard for it. All my brave Germans have.' Then he had stamped his right foot down hard in triumph and had peered out of the great picture window into the glowing darkness, as if out there he could see those great German warriors of old whom he believed guided his destiny.

He returned his attention to his gross-looking secretary, with his bull-like neck and heavy jowl who looked like a boxer gone to seed, and repeated, 'A symbol, Bormann . . . a sign . . . a token of Germany's strength. Soon our armies in Russia will march again once this winter is over. Then they will finally slay the Bolshevik beast. But my brave soldiers in the east need a symbol, one that will inspire them and one that the Reds and the cowardly Anglo-Saxons, skulking in their little island, will understand fully. It will symbolize the unbeatable might of German arms and demonstrate that the holy creed of the New Order cannot be stopped.' He paused momentarily, his cheeks flushed with excitement. 'Bormann, it must be . . . be something,' he stuttered as he tried to find the words to express the depth of his feelings, 'that will transcend all time, that will be remembered when you and I have long passed on . . .' He gasped for breath. 'Do you understand, Bormann?'

'Yes, I understand, *mein Führer*,' the secretary said hastily, though in reality he didn't. He attempted to match Hitler's excitement. 'You speak, sir, as if you intend to conquer nature itself.'

'*Genau, Bormann*,' Hitler agreed eagerly. 'That is exactly what I mean. The conquest of nature itself, something that we Germans alone can do. No other race has the daring, the imagination, to do so.' He peered out at the darkness and the white peak of the Watzmann mountain beyond, as if he sought inspiration there. 'For instance an achievement like the ascent of some hitherto unclimbed mountain,' he ventured. 'What a symbol that would make! How it would impress the rest of the world.' His eyes blazed fanatically as he warmed to the new idea. Impatient, though he didn't show it, Bormann waited for him to finish exploring his crazy idea. The new teleprinter operator in his office, the girl with all that wood before the house door*, went off duty soon. She was obviously panting for it. He'd pleasure her before she went off duty.

Nature submitting to the heroic creed of the National Socialist New Order. The echoes of such a conquest of tremendous proportions would reach even the remotest village in the furthest corner of the world. Hitler swung round to face his secretary, his face crazy with excitement. 'Bormann, I implore you . . . find me a mountain to conquer.'

*German slang expression for a large bosom. *Transl.*

4

Two

Five hundred kilometres to the west, Sergeant Schulze of Wotan's Company C heard the sound first. He was slumped in the freezing thunderbox outside his *isba* being sick into his helmet. At first he thought the noise came from his fellow New Year revellers inside the Russian hut but, drunk as he was, the big NCO of the SS's premier regiment knew that couldn't be. There was something furtive, sinister about the sound outside.

Schulze forgot his rumbling exploding guts, the result of a case of good Munich suds and two bottles of Russki firewater. He clapped his helmet on his big shaven head, the vomit running unheeded down his face, and grabbed his machine pistol hanging from a nail to his right. Even when Wotan troopers went to the thunderbox, they always carried their weapons with them. After six months in Russia, they had learned just how cunning the Popovs were.

Moving with surprising stealth for such a big man, he eased himself out of the privy, crouched in the freezing darkness and searched his surrounds by the spectral light of the sickle moon, as it skidded between the clouds.

For a few moments he couldn't spot anything and thought he had been mistaken. Perhaps it had been the firewater. But then, he heard the strange sound again. A faint slithering across the surface of the frozen snow, almost like the sound rats make when they are disturbed in the darkness of a sewer.

But then, he told himself, rats didn't come on two legs. For inbetween the parked Mark IV tanks of C Company, he caught a fleeting glimpse of a hunched figure in white moving swiftly and virtually noiselessly towards von Dodenburg's

5

command tank. It was easily identifiable by its two aerials, now sparkling white with hoar frost.

The SS sergeant hesitated. The clang of metal against metal made him move fast in the next instant. He recognized the sound immediately. Someone had just attached a magnetic mine to the CO's tank. He raised his machine pistol and, without aiming, fired a swift burst into the sky, at the same time yelling at the top of his voice, '*Alarm . . . alarm . . . die Ivans greifen an . . . Ala—*'

The urgent cry died on his lips as yet another of the strange hunched figures came hurtling past Schulze. This time the big SS NCO was ready for the attacker. He flung up his Schmeisser. In the same instant he fired a burst. White tracer bullets cut the darkness lethally. The figure crumpled. It screamed as it fell, shrill, high and hysterical like a woman might. Propelled forwards as if by a gigantic fist, the figure slammed into the nearest Mark IV. Von Dodenburg's command tank rose from the ground with a muffled roar before falling; as the 30-ton tank hit the ground it burst into flame instantly. Inside its turret ammunition started to explode. Shells zig-zagged crazily into the night sky. Schulze could see the hurrying figures everywhere, hunched in their white snow-capes as they sped effortlessly forward on their oiled skis.

Suddenly all was controlled violence. Half-naked Wotan troopers, pulling up their trousers, flung themselves into the snow outside their *isbas*, snapping off shots to left and right. The whores that some of the men had smuggled into C Company lines ran, screaming and panic-stricken, into the night to be felled by the wild shooting of the men who had been their loves only minutes before.

Captain von Dodenburg, C Company's CO, roused by the crazy fire-fight took charge. Armed with a pistol, he pushed his way to the forefront of the rough-and-ready Wotan firing line. With the arrogant, reckless bravery which had made him known throughout the Armed SS, he cried, 'All right, you hounds from hell, do you want to live for ever? On your feet, brave lads . . . Let's get the Ivan bastards before they knock out another of our tanks. *Los . . . Dalli . . . dalli—*'

6

Almost as if to emphasize the urgency of the young CO's order, another Mark IV exploded. Its ten-ton turret rose three or four metres into the air. There it turned a lazy somersault. Out of the mashed turret, smoke arose in a lazy ring as if from some giant cigar.

Von Dodenburg had no time for the dramatic end of the tank. He rushed forward, not knowing whether his men were going to follow him or not. One of the camouflaged figures on skis attempted to whizz by him, between two tanks. Von Dodenburg was quicker than the Russian. He didn't appear to aim, instead he fired from the hip. The figure screamed. Again its cry was strangely female. The Russian went down in a flailing chaos of arms and skis. As von Dodenburg ran by the Russian, writhing in the snow, von Dodenburg shot him in the face. By now he had learned never to take chances with Russians. The enemy skier lay still.

By now Schulze was rallying the more hesitant of the Wotan troopers. 'Come on, you piss pansies,' he yelled against the crazy background of the fire-fight. 'What yer waiting for – a frigging invitation to the dance. Get in ter the Popov barnshitters . . . *Ran wie Bluecher*!'

His words worked. With a wild roar the Wotan troopers surged forward. Carried away with the unreasoning blood lust of battle, they sought out the Russians still trying to attach the bombs to the steel sides of the Mark IVs. No mercy was given or expected. They slashed and hacked at each other. Rifle-butts, shovels, knives, brass knuckles, claws were all used by men determined to kill come what may; men turned into savages, with their eyes bulging from their sockets as if they were demented.

How long that desperate struggle went on, no one remembered later. As suddenly and startlingly as they had come, the attackers broke and fled, hushing in to the night on their waxed skis, vanishing into the darkness and the mountains, almost before the Wotan troopers realized that they had dispersed.

It was then that Corporal Matz, Schulze's wizened-faced running mate, called, 'Hey Schulze, come and take a look at this, will ya?'

'Take a look at what?' Schulze yelled back in irritation, for he wanted to get down to the usual business of looting the Soviet dead before the other troopers got to the bodies – slumped in the unnatural postures of the violently done to death – first.

'This you arse with ears, never seen anything like it in my born days. 'The Popov that the CO just shot dead has got tits.'

'What?'

'You heard me. The dead Popov's got tits . . .'

Major Geier, the Vulture, stroked his huge beak of a nose which had given him his nickname. He was the head of SS Assault Battalion, Wotan. As he stared at the woman's body, he said, 'I wonder why, von Dodenburg . . . I wonder why.' He frowned as if he were puzzled.

It was now dawn. Despite the fact that it was bone-chilling cold outside, and fresh snow was beginning to drift down silently in sad little flakes, the Wotan troopers didn't seek the warm shelter of their own *isbas*. Instead they clustered around the open door of the one containing the body, sipping their 'nigger sweat', as they called their coffee, and spooning 'old man' tinned meat, reputedly made from the bodies of elderly men from Berlin's old folks homes, from their canteens; the steam wreathing up about their red-nosed faces. They, too, were as puzzled as Major Geier.

The Vulture took his time examining the naked body of the Russian woman, occasionally prodding her arms and thighs as if testing their muscular strength. Not that he was sexually interested in her. His tastes lay elsewhere. He pre-fered the pretty boys with powdered faces and plucked eyebrows who plied their wares outside Berlin's main stations.

Finally he seemed to have seen enough. He took the monocle he affected from his eye and polished away the steam, commanding, 'All right, von Dodenburg, close the door and get rid of those damned idle soldiers of yours. You'd think they'd have something else to do than stand there in the cold, gawping like a bunch of village idiots.'

'*Jawohl, Obersturmbannführer*,' von Dodenburg barked. He knew just how much the Vulture, a one hundred percent Prussian if there ever was one, loved military bullshit. He raised his voice, 'Sergeant Schulze, wheel those damned spectators away if you would . . . double-quick time.'

Schulze, as curious as the rest, but as always supportive of his beloved company commander especially when the hated Vulture was present, bellowed, '*Los*, you perverted banana-suckers. Move yer asses . . . at the double now.'

As von Dodenburg closed the door, Schulze winked and then he, too, vanished with the rest of the disappointed crowd.

The Vulture waited till they had finally gone, slapping his comic oversized riding breeches with the cane that he also affected, before he finally spoke. 'Look,' he started, pointing his cane at the dead girl's muscular thighs and then at her upper arms. 'Fine physical type. Obviously used to skiing. Not the usual kind of poor physical types the Ivans use when they send in cannonfodder in these spoiling attacks, the kind you experienced last night.'

Von Dodenburg nodded his cropped blond head, but said nothing.

'So why were you honoured,' he smiled briefly in that supercilious manner of his which always irritated von Dodenburg, 'by the attention of such top-class physical types, eh, von Dodenburg?'

Von Dodenburg wasn't going to give the Vulture the satisfaction of seeing him stumble through an answer to a question which puzzled him too. Instead he asked a question of his own. 'I might ask, sir,' he said, 'why has my C Company been placed in such an exposed position in the first place? This position should be held by infantry, not by the elite of the SS's armour, sir, in my humble opinion.' The Vulture concealed his annoyance. He said, 'Your opinion is in no way important, von Dodenburg, and you know it. But it *is* justified. And yesterday I was going to signal *Reichsführer SS* Himmler about the matter. After all, with certain exceptions, we're not going to use our armour in an offensive manner till the winter breaks and that won't be for weeks yet. So why keep us and the rest of the II Panzer Corps SS up here so close to the front?'

He paused and let his words sink in. 'Fortunately I did not send that signal. You know what a touchy soul *Reichsführer SS* is. He harbours grudges, too.' The Vulture's ugly face broke into a cynical smile. 'And I must not prejudice my chances of obtaining those general's stars, which are my aim, before this war is over.' His smile broadened and von Dodenburg knew it was a direct challenge to him to make some comment. He didn't. He knew that the Vulture had only joined the Waffen SS back in 1939 from the regular army because promotion in the SS was quicker. He had no feeling for the New Order, which intended to re-shape an old and decadent Europe into a blazing tribute to the holy creed of National Socialist Germany.

When von Dodenburg didn't rise to the bait, the Vulture continued, 'You see before I could do so, Himmer sent me one. In it he requested you should fly to the Führer's headquarters at Berchtesgaden immediately.'

For the first time, von Dodenburg was really shocked. The Führer wanted him at his mountain headquarters. Why? He usually summoned officers of his SS to Berchtesgaden to award them the German state's highest orders for bravery such as the Knight's Cross of the Iron Cross, which already hung around his neck. But Wotan had not been engaged in any serious fighting since the winter offensive which had fizzled out without victory for Germany.

The Vulture seemed to be able to read the younger officer's mind. He gave that brittle derisive laugh of his and commented, 'Never fear. I am sure, von Dodenburg, that before this war is over or you are making a handsome corpse in some God-forsaken bit of Russian earth, you'll cure your throatache* once more.'

Von Dodenburg opened his mouth to ask for an explanation, but the Vulture, his smile vanishing abruptly, cut him off with, 'Top Secret, von Dodenburg, can't tell you more

*As the range of Iron Cross decorations were worn on a ribbon around the recipient's throat, the slang expression for the winner of the award was to 'cure one's throatache'.

than you are reporting to the Führer within the next forty-eight hours. In the meantime your Company C will move to the rear. Apparently it has served its purpose as a decoy.' He touched his cane to his cap, set in the rakish angle of the SS, and added, 'You are to take two senior NCOs with you . . . and yes, the body is to be packed in ice and it goes with you as well. That's all. Bye.'

With that he was gone, leaving von Dodenburg staring at the naked body of the dead Russian woman in complete, total bewilderment.

Three

The Bavarian inn was crowded with bronzed soldiers of the High Mountain Corps, their tough healthy faces glazed with sweat as the ceiling high, green tiled *Kachelofen* blazed away at full blast, turning the *Bierstube* into a hothouse. Outside the storm raged noisily, as the snowflakes hit the place's tiny windows like tracer and the wind surged down from the Alps with a banshee-like howl.

The mountain troopers didn't mind. They were safe and warm inside the inn, today's climb had been cancelled for some reason or other and the CO, Colonel Sturmer, had personally paid for two rounds of good Munich beer out of his own pocket. The big-bosomed country maids, in their low-cut *dirndls*, hurried back and forth cradling eight or ten steins of foaming suds to their massive breasts, expertly dodging the importuning hands which attempted to grope under the layers of their white petticoats to pinch their ample, so tempting bottoms.

Colonel Sturmer sat next to his second-in-command, Major Greul, sipping a white wine, while Greul, puritan that he was, drank a *sprudel** believing a good soldier must remain hard at all times. Sturmer allowed his gaze to roam around the *bierstube*, decorated with the usual dusty antlers, the obligatory crucifix – for the local peasants were still very pious despite the Nazis – and a faded picture depicting a naughty little boy pissing into a puddle of water. Below the picture it bore the traditional warning, Never Drink Water.

Sturmer's big tough face cracked into a smile and he looked around at his men. Happy and by now slightly drunk, they

*Sparkling water. *Transl.*

12

looked good to him, relaxed after being withdrawn from Russia. The High Mountain Corps had suffered terrible casualties there during the last three months, before the German winter offensive had ended in failure – thank God.

Although he commanded a battalion of some five hundred of the best alpinists in the *Wehrmacht*, Sturmer hated war as much as he loved the high mountains. He loved the physical effort, the constant danger, the skill and craft needed, the wealth of memories of fellow climbers who didn't make it. He liked, too, the responsibility they had unwittingly thrust upon him to carry out the tasks they had been unable to finish: the responsibility for good, brave men, who had to be commanded and led, not by orders, but by example, which was real leadership.

But most of all the colonel felt the high mountains conferred dignity and freedom on him, far removed from the loud, jackbooted, cheap vulgarity of the National Socialist '1,000 Reich' to which he now belonged: a clean wholesomeness, wrapped in the brooding silence of the deep, eternal snow, which even the Brownshirts couldn't spoil.

As he sat there next to Greul, the epitome of all he disliked in the new Nazi creed, listening to the noise made by his happy, half-tipsy men, he felt *his* mountains were the last refuge from the evil tide of arrogant aggression which had engulfed the whole of continental Europe since 1939. The high mountains were the final escape.

'Sir . . . Colonel Sturmer.' Greul's harsh north German voice cut into his happy reverie.

'Yes.' He shook himself out of his dreamlike state with a jerk. 'Where's the fire, Greul?'

'The door, sir . . . SS,' Greul answered.

Three soldiers had entered the inn and were busy stamping their feet and shaking the snow off their greatcoats, which they had opened to reveal the silver runes of the SS. Their obvious leader, a tall lean young officer with a harshly handsome face under his rakishly tilted cap, was looking around the crowded smoke-filled *bierstube* with the arrogant superior look of the Waffen SS, as if Sturmer's mountaineers, every man an expert at his craft, were members of an inferior race.

13

But there was no denying the force, even menace in the SS officer's pale blue eyes. If the half-drunk mountain soldiers didn't recognize it, the barmaids did. As busy as they were, hurrying back and forth with the great steins of beer for Sturmer's troops, they made careful circles around the SS men at the door, doing a little country curtsey whenever they got close to the SS officers. Here in the Berchtesgaden, within sight of the Führer's own mountain home, they knew all about the SS and what happened to those who incurred their wrath.

Sturmer finished his wine and rose from his hard-backed wooden chair. The officer turned to face him and appeared to take a long time to recognize the fact that Sturmer was also an officer and indeed one who outranked him by several grades. As Sturmer pushed his way through the mob to the door, he told himself it was typical of the SS. They were a law to themselves and regarded the *Wehrmacht* as an inferior part of Germany's fighting forces.

The SS officer finally deigned to recognize the fact that he was being approached by a superior officer. Slowly he raised his hand to the gleaming peak of his cap and, as he did so, Sturmer noted the Knight's Cross of the Iron Cross dangling from his throat, beneath the snow-covered greatcoat. Behind their leader two NCOs clicked to attention.

The sound of their boots stamping on the wooden floor caught the attention of Sturmer's mountaineers. They stopped their drinking, some of them with their steins poised stupidly at their mouths, as if they couldn't believe what they were seeing. Ox-Jo, Sturmer's senior sergeant, renowned for his ox-like strength, hence his nickname, wiped his big paw across his mouth and growled, 'By Christ's blood, the Prussians have arrived, boys!' Sturmer frowned briefly. He knew his Bavarian mountaineers. They traditionally hated what they called 'sow-Prussians'. Given half a chance and a few beers inside them, they'd be fighting these new arrivals at the drop of a hat.

The SS captain snapped rigidly to attention as if he were still a new recruit on the barracks square, though his dangerous blue eyes continued to fix the other officer,

'*Hauptsturmführer von Dodenburg,*' he barked, '*SS Sturm-battalion Wotan, mit zwei Mann, Herr Oberstleutnant!*'

Casually Sturmer nodded his acknowledgement and said, 'Sturmer, *Gebirgsjäger Zwo.*' He reached out his hand. The young SS officer took it formally and pressed it with a hand that felt as cold as death.

Sturmer nodded to one of the barmaids, 'Something to drink for our visitors,' he called. His own men went back to their beer and schnapps. Behind von Dodenburg, Schulze turned to his running mate, Matz, the Bavarian barnshitter as Schulze called him, and said, 'You frigging Bavarian yokels don't do too bad for folk who ain't got a pot to piss in – beer for breakfast! Now that's what I call style.'

Matz, the little Bavarian, wasn't offended. He whispered back as the two officers went back to Sturmer's table, 'Keep it down to a low roar, Schulzi, old comrade. You're in outlaw country up here, you know. Bavarians are a rum lot. They'd punch out yer choppers as soon as they'd look at you.'

Schulze continued to grin. 'Don't piss yer pants about me, Matzi, I think stubble-hoppers who drink beer for breakfast can't be all bad.'

Sturmer waited till von Dodenburg had downed his schnaps in one gulp, the fashion of regular officers, before he said, keeping his voice low, 'So you're involved in this business as well, von Dodenburg, eh?' He nodded to Greul and the latter signalled to the barmaid for another round of schnaps.

The SS officer looked puzzled. 'Seemingly,' he answered. 'All I know is that I was summoned to Berchtesgaden forty-eight hours ago with two of my best NCOs, and when I arrived I was informed to report to the High Mountain Corps in Bad Reichenhall. From there I was dispatched to meet you, sir. I believe you've been on a climbing exercise. That's about it.' He stopped abruptly and looked at Sturmer expectantly.

Sturmer cleared his throat. 'I can't enlighten you very much, von Dodenburg,' he commenced, gazing across at the two SS NCOs who were now seated with a group of his tipsy mountaineers. The latter were gazing at the SS men as

15

if they were creatures from another world, which, in a way, they were. 'As you know we won't go over to the offensive again in the East until the winter is virtually over. One doesn't need to be a crystal-gazer to realize that the *Wehrmacht* is preparing for a final spring offensive which should break the Popovs once and for all.'

Von Dodenburg nodded his agreement.

Over at the other table, Schulze was being initiated into the brutal art of finger wrestling by the Bavarian giant, Ox-Jo. Sturmer said a quick prayer that the game wouldn't get out of hand. Ox-Jo had an explosive temper like most Bavarians.

'However,' Sturmer continued as he took his gaze away from the two giants, 'the High Mountain Corps, in particular my battalion, have been put on red alert, to be ready within twenty-four hours, to depart for the front in the East in the area of the Caucasus Mountains. Rumour has it in Bad Reichenhall that your Reichsführer SS has given that order to the corps personally. Now,' he looked hard at von Dodenburg, 'you of the SS turn up here in the mountains, although you are the member of an armoured regiment of the SS. What is the link?'

Von Dodenburg hesitated. He realized that Sturmer was no time-server of a *Wehrmacht* officer, who had picked the Mountain Corps because, although it was a tough physical assignment, it didn't suffer the same horrific casualties that the ordinary stubble-hoppers of the infantry did. The decorations which adorned his simple grey tunic indicated that the Colonel had seen his share of action. He decided to play his hand with open cards. 'It has puzzled me, too, Colonel. Why should an armoured regiment be placed in the front line, as is the case with Wotan, when there is no need for armour there at the moment and why now? Is there to be some kind of co-operation? I can't think of another example of an armoured unit being linked to a mountain one, can you, sir?'

Sturmer shook his head, while Greul looked from one to the other of the two officers, as if he wondered why all this discussion. After all, his battalion of troops must be going

16

to work together with the SS's most celebrated regiment, the one they called the Führer's Fire Brigade because it was always sent where the front was at its hottest. Sturmer, Greul told himself, should be honoured by the association. What good Nazi wouldn't be.

'Gentlemen,' he interrupted, 'I wonder if we ought to discuss this problem any further, especially in a common inn with all the men listening. Surely we will know our mission, if there is to be one, soon enough when the time comes. *Reichsführer SS* Himmler surely has his good reasons for not letting us know the mission just yet.'

Von Dodenburg looked at the pompous second-in-command and decided then and there that he didn't like him. He didn't know why. The man did indeed carry party decorations on his tunic which indicated that he was a member of the National Socialist Party, still he didn't like him. He turned to Colonel Sturmer to ascertain his reaction to Greul's words.

'Well,' the latter said, 'a little bird at headquarters down in Bad Reichenhall has twirped to me that will be the last forty-eight hour alert period we will enjoy. After that we will be gone so—' The big mountain colonel stopped short abruptly.

Over at Ox-Jo's table the big Bavarian was grunting and panting hard, the veins on his forehead standing out like purple wires, as he forced the SS's hand slowly but inexorably down to the white scrubbed surface of the table, both men pressing their feet down hard like anchors as they attempted to exert their last reserves of strength.

Sturmer knew he couldn't allow Ox-Jo to win. He didn't want bad blood between these 'sow-Prussians' of the SS and his own Bavarians right from the start. If the two units were going to work together, this was not the way to begin. Finger wrestling, as his Bavarians saw it, was not a game; it was a war. '*Oberjager Mayr*,' he commanded harshly rising to his feet, 'enough of that!'

Ox-Jo paused, his chest heaving, gasping for breath. In that same instant, Sergeant Schulze exerted the last of his strength. Caught completely off guard, Ox-Jo lurched forward. His big head slammed against the table top and he yelped with

17

pain. A crimson-faced Schulze let go of his hand and, staggering to his feet, grabbed his opponent's glass of beer and poured it over his head, crying, '*Los*, you don't want to be out for the count, comrade, do you?'

Matz acted quickly. He knew his fellow countrymen's hair-trigger tempers. He grabbed Schulze by the tail of his greatcoat, hissing, 'Park your stupid fat arse, Schulze. In three devils' name sit down and shut up or they'll have the balls off'n yer with a blunt bayonet in zero, comma, nothing, seconds.'

Von Dodenburg groaned as the Bavarian mountaineers all around him looked at the triumphant NCO, eyes blazing with anger. He told himself that Wotan was not going to get on with these Bavarians, if this was any example. There would be blood spilled in the end.

Sturmer must have thought the same. He turned to Greul swiftly and commanded, 'Get the men outside, Major . . . double quick time. *Dalli* . . . *dalli* . . . We're going back to Bad Reichenhall.'

As the men filed out, grabbing their carbines purposefully as if they might well use them on the sow-Prussians, muttering sullenly as they did so, Colonel Sturmer turned to von Dodenburg. He forced a smile. 'Don't worry, *Hauptsturmbannführer*. It looks worse than it is. We'll get on together, your people and mine, after all we are *all* Germans.'

Von Dodenburg returned the mountaineer's smile, telling himself he, personally, would get on with the colonel, but he didn't know about the others.

Together they went outside into the falling snow and watched as the mountain troops formed up; the muleteers pushing and shoving the awkward pack mules, laden with the Battalion's heavy equipment, into some form of order. At the head of the column, Major Greul shouted, '*Marsch*'. The column set off with Schulze and Matz trailing a little behind, wisely so, von Dodenburg couldn't help thinking. And it was then that Sturmer sprang his surprise, one that indicated to von Dodenburg that the mountain colonel had already taken to him. 'Von Dodenburg,' he said, when his men were out of earshot, 'try to find a *Duden* or better a

Brockhaus in Bad Reichenhall. Check if you can which is the highest mountain in the Caucasus. That might solve your problem somewhat.'

Von Dodenburg turned and stared at Sturmer very puzzled. 'I don't understand, sir. What exactly—'

'Just find one of those reference books I've just mentioned, von Dodenburg.' He pulled up his collar against the falling snow. 'Come on, I'll buy you a *Glühwein* in the Mess.'

And with that a puzzled Kuno von Dodenburg had to be contented.

Four

'Hairy-arsed Bavarian bastards,' Schulze growled, as they watched Sturmer's mountaineers go through their paces along the rock face. 'I mean, you need yer head sorting out wanting to climb up those mountains – and with a sixty pound rucksack on yer back as well. The silly arseholes haven't got the sense they were born with. Bavarians!' He spat contemptuously into the snow, which was still falling from the sky as if it would never stop.

Matz looked worried. He wanted to support his old running mate, but at the same time he was proud of Bavaria, where he had been born. 'Don't go rabbiting on like that, Schulzi, for God's sake. They'll hear you. All us Bavarians are brought up with the snow and mountains. We suck it in with our mother's titty.'

Schulze looked down at Matz disdainfully. 'Good job you've had me to look after you all this time. At least I've civilized yer. *Bavarians*!' Again he spat into the snow.

'Now,' Ox-Jo was bellowing – he seemed always to talk at the top of his voice, even now, when his listeners were a matter of metres away, 'you men, most of the pitches we've dealt with have been routine. Yer don't need much skill – or strength – to master them 'cept the usual knee-jam, friction old, the old press-and-push—'

'What in hell's name is he talking about, Matzi?' Schulze asked the smaller man, as Ox-Jo used his hands like small steam shovels to demonstrate a climber's techniques.

Matz shrugged eloquently. 'We didn't have much in the way of mountains in the slums of Munich where I was brought up, Schulzi. Great crap on the Christmas tree, how should I know what he's babbling on about? Watch and find out.'

'But not many of you have tried to do the pendulum. Now, Major Greul here is going to show how a professional tackles it.' Ox-Jo stepped back and extended a hand to the big lean major who had climbed his first eight thousand metre height as a sixteen year old member of the Hitler Youth and who had tackled the north face of the Eiger in his twentieth year.

Greul didn't hesitate. He reached up, hammered a piton home in the rock, let the hammer which dangled from a loop on his right wrist fall, and carefully exerted his full weight on the steel hook. Below him there was drop of some hundred metres between two rock faces. The hook held.

He paused momentarily and then, with expert swiftness, he ran a length of climbing rope, anchored by Ox-Jo, through a snap ring and fastened the loop to his waist.

Schulze's mouth dropped open like that of gawping village yokel and he breathed, 'You don't tell me that the silly swine is going—' He never finished his words, for in that instant Greul took one last hasty look at Ox-Jo braced on the narrow rock ledge above him and launched himself into space.

'Holy strawsack!' Schulze exclaimed. 'He must be mad. What's he want – a shitting idiot's grave?'

Far below, watching the proceedings through his binoculars on the roof of the mountain troops' Bad Reichenhall barracks, von Dodenburg whistled his admiration. He didn't particularily like Greul, but he had to admire his courage. The man obviously knew what he was on about. All the same, at this very moment he was dangling above a fearsome drop, spinning like a top, legs seeking some sort of a hold so that he could continue his demonstration to the watching mountain troops. Von Dodenburg told himself he'd rather tackle a couple of Ivan T-34 tanks head-on than do what Greul was doing.

He took his eyes off the demonstration of mountain climbing skills and flashed a look at the open copy of the *Volksbrockhaus* that he had obtained second-hand in Bad Reichenhall. Hastily his eyes skimmed the short entry full of abbreviations, but still complete enough to give him an idea of what lay in front of Sturmer's mountain men and presumably his own too; though for the life of him he couldn't

21

imagine what Wotan's armour might be doing in the Caucasus Mountains.

'*Elbrus*,' he read, '*hochster Berg des Kaukasus. 5642 m.**
. . . located in tribal areas of Karatski, centered on the village of Chursuk.' There was a small line map but it revealed nothing and, as von Dodenburg considered what their mountain exercise might be, he told himself that he had to find a large scale map of the area. This might prove difficult. Since Germany had invaded Russia in the summer of 1941, large-scale maps had proved difficult to find; the military had bought them all up or the local party authorities had removed them from the shops so that their citizens couldn't see just how much terrain the *Wehrmacht* would have to conquer to achieve final victory in that accursed land.

Greul had completed the pendulum successfully. Breathing a little harder, he now wedged his lithe body between the rock faces. Next to Schulze, Matz whispered, 'That's what they call a chimney . . . I know that at least.'

Schulze sniggered. 'If that Major don't watch out, that chimney's gonna set his skinny arse afire.'

Ox-Jo heard the remark. He had already grown to dislike the big Wotan NCO with his sharp Prussian tongue and cocky manner. He said threateningly, in his thick Bavarian accent, 'You watch your lips, apeturd or I might just pass yer a knuckle sandwich.' He clenched his big fist to make his meaning quite clear.

Schulze raised his middle finger; it looked like a hairy sausage.

'You know what you can do with that, comrade,' he said.

Ox-Jo flushed crimson. He took one step forward, but was stopped in his tracks as a corporal behind him barked, as if he were on parade, '*Achtung* . . . The colonel.'

Sturmer took the situation in immediately. 'Sergeant,' he snapped to Ox-Jo, 'that's enough. Now, what's going on here?'

Ox-Jo clicked to attention. 'Major Greul is tackling the chimney, sir.'

'Did he do the pendulum first, Sergeant?'

'Yessir.'

---

*'Elbrus: highest mountain in the Caucasus. 5642 metres.' *Transl.*

Sturmer cursed under his breath. He controlled his temper with difficulty, as he bent down and peered down the chimney.

Greul, some fifty metres below, was finding the going tough, but not beyond his strength. Palms and back against one rock face, mountain boots dug into the other, he was making good progress, levering himself downwards, metre by metre, heading for the spot where the chimney narrowed and the going would become more difficult.

Even experienced mountain climbers disliked a narrowing chimmey; it placed tremendous strain on the human body. But the men had to be shown how it was done and Greul discounted the strain. He had been punishing and hardening his lean body with an almost religious intensity ever since he had heard the clarion call of the new National Socialist creed as a teenager. Action was his motto, action which made the German male 'as strong as Krupp steel, as speedy as a greyhound and as tough as leather,' as the Party creed expressed it.

At that moment an angry Colonel Sturmer was not concerned with Greul's efforts to prove himself the ideal National Socialist soldier. He was more interested in protecting the fool's life at this crucial preliminary stage of the new mission. He needed experienced officers like Greul; for what he had already learned of the operation, it would be difficult, damnably difficult. He clapped his hands over the sides of his mouth and shouted down the chimney. 'Major Greul, you are to come up this very instant. I won't have you risking your life any further.' He nodded to Ox-Jo. 'Haul him up at once.'

Greul heard the command and looking up, face strained and red, cried, 'I don't need assistance, sir . . . I can make my own way up.'

Sturmer knew that his order had deeply offended Greul's sense of honour, his vanity even. Real mountaineers were never hauled up a chimney; that was the way that frightened recruits, who had frozen with fear and couldn't move either up or down were dealt with. Sturmer ignored Greul's cry. Instead he snapped angrily at Ox-Jo, 'Don't just stand there, man. Start pulling the Major up. *At once!*'

The big Bavarian NCO, who was one of Greul's few

favourites in the battalion, exerted his great muscles. Single-handedly he started to haul Greul up and whether he liked it or not, Major Greul had to submit to the indignity, pulling in his legs and relaxing the grip his back had had on the opposite rock wall, if he didn't want to hurt himself.

A few minutes later, with Ox-Jo panting heavily, he appeared over the side of the crevice, his eyes blazing in anger, and stumbled to attention in front of a grim-faced and equally angry Colonel Sturmer. Watching the two of them through his binoculars, von Dodenburg could see that something had gone wrong. The two officers' body language made that quite clear even though he couldn't hear what they were saying to each other. He lowered the glasses slowly and frowned. He was as careful of his men's lives as he thought Sturmer was of his men and he guessed Greul, just like the Vulture, would be an officer who would put personal advancement in front of the safety of his men. Still he was not concerned with Sturmer's unit. He was too concerned about his own men. Obviously the two units were going to be sent off on some wild mission in the Caucasus mountains and von Dodenburg felt worried about how well the two groups would work together. '*Elbrus, hochster Berg des Kaukasus. 5642 m.*' The words of the *Volksbrockhaus* flashed through his mind again. What kind of crazy venture was this going to be?

It was roughly the same kind of thought that occupied the minds of the two old running mates, Schulze and Matz, at that moment. They contemplated the two officers facing each other, red-faced and angry, their fists clenched as if they might launch an attack on each other. Out of the side of his mouth, Matz whispered, 'I told yer, Schulzi, that Bavarians have got hot tempers, but this little lot, well—' He shrugged his skinny shoulders and left the rest of his sentence unsaid, as if he had said enough already.

Ox-Jo, standing close by and also watching the two angry officers, turned abruptly and said to Matz, 'You a Bavarian, you short-arsed piss-pansy? . . . You're never a Bavarian in a million years. And you,' he looked challengingly at Schulze, 'I've warned you already. One more word out of you and you'll be lacking a set of front teeth, very smartish.'

Schulze flushed and took a step forward. Matz grabbed him just in time. 'Ignore the big prick,' he urged, 'he doesn't know who he's talking to. *Grosser Gott*, he's risking his very life talking to Sergeant Schulze, the pride of the SS NCO Corps, like that.'

Ox-Jo was unimpressed. He raised his right leg and ripped off a long and contemptuous fart, a big grin all over his ugly face. 'Take a ride on that, pride of the SS NCO Corps – while yer safe.'

Schulze shook off Matz's grip but it was too late. The mountain troops were already forming up to march back to the barracks in the little Bavarian town below. The damage had been done however. Schulze knew he had made an implacable enemy in Ox-Jo and he, too, wanted his revenge. Soon the time would come to square accounts.

Up on the flat roof of the barracks, von Dodenburg replaced his binoculars in their case and picked up the book. He sensed, rather than knew, that something had gone wrong in the mountains above. As he started to clatter down the stairs into the interior of the nineteenth century barracks he heard Schulze's old phrase shooting back and forth in his brain; 'Buy combs lads – there are lousy times ahead . . .'

25

Five

' *Heil Hitler,*' General Dietl, commander of the II Mountain Corps, greeted the three officers as he entered the briefing room, giving them the Hitler greeting which was not customary in the *Wehrmacht*

Naturally Greul, the fervent Nazi, threw up a magnificent salute, while von Dodenburg, an officer in Hitler's own SS, did the same, though not so fervently. Sturmer contented himself with the old mountaineer's greeting, '*Berg Heil*', without a raised hand.

Dietl, who had been instrumental in conquering Norway back in 1940 and who had enjoyed Hitler's favour ever since, frowned but said nothing. After all, Sturmer was a mountaineer with an international reputation; he needed officers like the colonel for what was to come. 'Please be seated, gentlemen, we have a lot to discuss this afternoon.'

Dietl threw his peaked ski cap, with the Edelweiss badge of the Mountain Corps, on the table and announced without any further preliminaries, 'Well, we've got it, gentlemen.' His craggy skinny face beamed. 'I knew we would. And what an honour.'

Greul was the only one of his three listeners who showed enthusiasm. He exclaimed, 'My God, sir, can it be true? *The mountain?*'

'Yes it can, Greul.' Without pausing Dietl turned to von Dodenburg and said, 'You're new to this kind of business, *Hauptsturmbannführer*. Let me fill you in.' He pointed to the big map of Central Russia, which Greul had set out for this key briefing. 'At present, von Dodenburg, our troops in Russia are spread out in a somewhat loose front from the River Kuban – here in the north – and to the Black Sea, here in the south. We are poised at the entrance to the Caucasus. And as you can see from our dispositions and what we know of the Russian ones, the front is very porous. There are plenty of gaps to slip through in smaller formations.'

Sturmer and von Dodenburg craned their heads forward. In the past both of them had used such gaps in a loosely-held front for their own advantage, in a flanking attack or in an encircling movement. 'Now, von Dodenburg, my corps have been used to stop the Russians from crossing the mountains and launching a flanking attack on our troops in the Black Sea. Once the spring offensive starts, in a couple of months, that will be our role once more. A somewhat boring and not very spectacular assignment.' He pulled a face as if he had just tasted something very unpleasant. Von Dodenburg thought to himself that Dietl was well known for his greed for publicity. Operating as a flank guard for an attacking army was not his idea of an assignment. He wanted one which would gain the newspaper headlines at home in the Reich.

Now Dietl turned his attention to the other two. 'However till that happens the Führer, in his infinite wisdom, has given some of us – you in particular Sturmer – the opportunity to gain even more glory for my II Mountain Corps.' He gave Sturmer a crafty lopsided smile.

Sturmer didn't react. Instead, he waited to hear what the assignment was, while von Dodenburg told himself the *Wehrmacht* must be full of senior officers like Dietl and his own CO Geier; eager for advancement over the dead bodies of their soldiers. He frowned.

'How is this to be achieved?' Dietl answered his own question. 'I shall tell you. So far our corps have carried out straightforward military assignments in Norway, Greece and Russia. Now we are to execute an operation – at the Führer's own specific request,' he added hastily as if it were very important, 'the like of which no German military unit has carried out in this war or any other as far as I know.' He wet his thin lips, as if they had become very dry. 'We are, gentlemen, to tackle what is in essence a peace time climb in the middle of total war. Not only will we be trying to overcome Mother Nature, we will also probably have to face problems with our enemies, the Ivans.'

Even von Dodenburg was impressed by the full magnitude of the mission, which Dietl had now revealed to them. Greul, for his part, could hardly restrain himself from jumping to his feet and yelling at the top of his voice '*Sieg Heil*'. His eyes blazed fanatically at the thought of what was to come. 'Sir, it will be a great honour. A peace time climb in the middle of war.'

'Agreed, Greul,' Dietl said and continued, 'As you know, Colonel Sturmer, Russia is forbidden territory for foreign climbers. Ever since the Reds had their revolution they have refused to allow outsiders to climb their mountains, some of which have still to be conquered. They have an almost pathological fear that foreign climbers might well be spies. So all we know about their climbs is what we can read from Soviet mountain literature and the experiences of foreign climbers in pre-revolutionary days. And that's not much. So any attempt on the Elbrus is like going on a journey into no-man's land.'

'But why the Elbrus?' Sturmer spoke for the first time. 'What value has the conquest of that mountain got in military terms?'

It was a question that von Dodenburg would have liked to have asked himself, but, as the junior officer present, he felt it was not right for him to do so. All the same he leaned forwards intently as Dietl started to explain.

The commander of the 2nd Mountain Corps tapped the map. 'Here stands Elbrus, with absolutely no military value whatsoever.' He looked sharply at Sturmer. 'The mountain has never been climbed by Germans. So why are we going to climb it in the middle of a war? Because it will be a symbol. One, for our own hard-pressed people, men and women, back on the homefront who have made so many sacrifices to ensure Germany's future victory. But there is more to it than that, gentlemen. Two, we must show the world that Germany now rules Europe. We can plant the German flag anywhere we wish and no one can stop us from doing so. This is the German century and our flag fluttering above Mount Elbrus will demonstrate that to one and all. Three, although the Soviets outnumber us in men and machines and, with our losses growing every year, we have no hope of ever catching up with the Reds, we shall convince them by this symbolic act that we are invincible and that they can never beat us.'

He paused and let his words sink in. Even the sceptic, von Dodenburg, felt a mounting sense of excitement at Dietl's words. He didn't know Wotan's role in this bold mission. It didn't matter. What mattered was the new hope that the proposed conquest of Mount Elbrus gave him, a new hope for the whole of Germany. The nation had been fighting too long, making too many sacrifices in blood and sweat. Anything that might bring the war in the East to a speedier end had to be welcomed with open arms.

Dietl realized that he had convinced the three officers, well at least the two younger ones, Greul and von Dodenburg. He continued excitedly, 'Yesterday I spoke to the Führer and he gave his personal blessing to our mission. He said, "Give me Mount Elbrus, Dietl, and I'll guarantee you that not only will the whole world realize that nothing can stop National Socialist Germany –" Dietl's faded blue eyes blazed suddenly, as if he were carried away by his own rhetoric – "but that the Elbrus Mountain will be the key to our conquest of the whole of Southern Russia. Carry out this bold blow with a handful of brave men, dedicated to our cause, and our Fatherland will capture all the oil there that we shall need to ensure final victory. Then our beloved flag will fly triumphantly over the whole of Europe, once and for all".'

He stopped abruptly, his skinny chest heaving with the effort of all that talking.

While the other two young officers' faces glowed with excitement at the prospect, Colonel Sturmer's remained stony. He didn't share the other three Nazis' vulgar dream: the conquest of Mount Elbrus's peak as a symbol of national superiority. The Elbrus project seemed to him to be yet another example of National Socialist Germany's elitist thinking. He cleared his throat and determined to try to stop this crazy adventure before it even got started. 'It is clear,

General, that my battalion will do our utmost to carry out the mission. But a problem has arisen, Herr General.'

Dietl smiled winningly at him. 'And what is that, my dear Colonel Sturmer?'

'This, sir. Intelligence reported to me that our serial reconnaissance stopped Russian troops on the Elbrus twenty-four hours ago.'

Dietl's look of self-satisfaction vanished. Opposite him, Greul caught his breath sharply. 'What did you say?'

Sturmer repeated himself, adding, 'And Herr General, what are we to make of that, sir?'

Dietl didn't answer. He couldn't. He had no answer ready for that particular, overwhelming question.

A heavy silence fell over the room, broken only by the voice of Ox-Jo drilling a bunch of new recruits, yelling at them in the traditional fashion, 'The captain's got a hole in his arse, follow me!' They followed, stamping across the parade ground in heavy, nailed mountain boots heading for the carefully prepared patch of mud where, in moments, Ox-Jo would inevitably order them to *hinlegen, aufstehen, hinlegen** till they were soaked in mud, their breath coming in sharp hectic gasps.

Watching Ox-Jo and his recruits, Schulze, who had been through the same sort of brutal drill in his time, commented, 'The poor devils might be dead before this month is out, but does that big Bavarian slime-shitter care? Does he hell!' He rasped heavily and spat angrily.

'It's always bin that way, Schulzi. Nothing you can do about it, old house.'

Schulze opened his mouth to object, but he didn't. For approaching them his gaze was suddenly taken by the sight of a tall handsome blonde, her plaits styled around her head in the Bavarian peasant fashion. In her basket, she carried what looked like two bottles of beer nestled in a clean towel, next to a large roll, stuffed with salami.

Schulze forgot Ox-Jo's training methods immediately. Taking off the peaked black cap of the SS, with its shining

*Down, up, down. *Transl.*

30

silver crossbones and death's head, he swept it in front of the woman and said gallantly, 'My name is Schulze, young miss. I am a very senior NCO in SS Assault Regiment Wotan – and I love you. Perhaps you will do me the great honour of visiting my quarters immediately. I have a gramophone. Perhaps we could dance or,' he winked knowingly, 'try some other form of physical activity.'

'God in heaven,' Matz muttered behind him. 'How vain can a man get!'

For a moment the Bavarian woman with the basket looked angry, then she had a closer look at the big imposing sergeant in his black armoured corps uniform, his broad chest covered with medals and smiled. 'You are very gallant, Sergeant,' she said without a trace of a Bavarian accent.

She wagged a finger at Schulze, who was beaming madly, while at his side Matz was beginning to look worried, for Ox-Jo had paused his training, leaving the poor recruits sprawled in the icy mud, and had turned in their direction. The blonde said, 'I know you naughty soldiers. I know what you're after. Two things – and the second one is food.'

Schulze laughed out loud. 'My God, a woman after my own heart. Matz, double away, dear comrade, and buy me a large bouquet of flowers – never mind the expense, you've got money – for this delightful lady, who might well be my betrothed before the week is out.'

But Schulze was slightly wrong in his calculations, for at that moment a great roar shattered the relative silence of the barracks square, as Ox-Jo took off his peaked cap and slamming it down to the ground, stamped upon it in a frenzy of overwhelming rage, crying, '*Himmelherrgottnochnal, was macht der Saupreuss mit meinem Madel?*'

'Shit!' Matz exclaimed at Ox-Jo's crazed outburst, 'now the tick-tock really is in the piss-pot, Schulze. For heaven's sake, leave the wench alone.'

Slowly, still with the gallant smile on his face, Schulze turned to see what all the fuss was about. 'Oh him,' he said, as a beetroot-red Ox-Jo continued to jump up and down, as if he were stamping his rival into the parade ground, and the recruits solidified in the freezing mud. 'Bit of a temper, what,' he said calmly. 'Funny lot of folk, you Bavarians.' He turned and addressed the tall blonde once more. 'May I take your basket, gracious lady – or may I call you my beloved?'

The big blonde's smile had gone. She looked worried. 'I am engaged – well, sort of – to Sergeant Mayr.'

Schulze dismissed her words with a careless wave of his big paw and took the basket with the beer off her. 'A temporary infatuation, my beloved,' he said lightly. 'Don't concern yourself with the matter in the slightest.' They swept from the parade ground, leaving Ox-Jo to rant and his recruits to feel they might well suffer frostbite if they didn't get out of the mud soon.

Matz, trotting behind the couple, noted her splendid arse and saw she was keeping tight control of the basket containing the beer, something which he admired in a woman. All the same, he told himself, soon things would have to come to a head between the two big NCOs and that Schulze knew little of the ways of Bavarians. You couldn't steal a Bavarian's girl that easily and when the bust up came, as it surely would, Bavarians didn't just use their fists and boots as they did in the North; Bavarians used a knife . . .

Six

The next thirty-six hours flew by. All normal duties were suspended as the men of the High Mountain Corps were placed on 'red alert' and concentrated on preparing for the new mission in Southern Russian, which was still being kept secret from them. Not that the veterans, 'the old hares', couldn't guess where they were heading. For the fact that they were being issued with special Arctic grease and oil, to prevent their weapons from seizing up and the lenses from fogging over, told them all they needed to know. 'It's Popovland again,' they whispered to each other, 'try to get yer leg over while yer can. You won't be seeing much in the way of beaver soon save them Popov mules.' No one laughed. All of them knew just how grim the Russian front was, especially when General Frost commanded in that God-forsaken waste land.

Colonel Sturmer had neither time for rumours nor to explain to his men what was coming. He was too much up to his eyeballs in preparations. For every hour of the day seemed to bring with it a fresh and major problem, from how much ammunition could he expect his men to carry to whether there was a need for salt tablets. Up in the Russian mountains, the sun would be terrific and in the thin, rarified air of the high slopes, he could expect heat exhaustion. Then there was the problem of how he should have his heavier supplies transported once they had left the vehicles of von Dodenburg's armoured column. Should he take mules to carry their portable mountain quick-firers? Was there a need for the little cannon? After all since the first alarming report that the Russians might be recceing the mountain, he had heard nothing else about Popov activity up there on the Elbrus.

Problem after problem occurred, so that at the end of a long exhausting day Sturmer would fall into his bunk, often without having eaten, to sleep till dawn, and his batman would have to shake him awake, feed him black coffee and schnapps so that he could face yet another gruelling day.

It was no different for the men. Though they each had a standard set of equipment, pack, weapon, bayonet, ice-axe, rope and the like, each man had his own particular favourite – a set of crampons, a well-worn *carbiner*, equipment that he felt he couldn't climb without – which somehow had to be fitted in. Then, before they set out on the climb, each man would be carefully checked to make sure he had not forgotten anything that might hold up progress or carried too much which could do the same thing. And they all knew that Ox-Jo had a keen eye for such things and a quick fist that punished those who incurred his wrath.

For Sergeant Schulze it was fortunate that Sturmer and his mountaineers, in particular Ox-Jo, were fully engaged in their preparations for the mission to come. As Schulze had explained to a worried Matz, 'I reckon Matzi, it'll only take another day and she'll be letting 'em down for yours truly very tout suite. Hannelore,' he said, talking of the blonde with the basket, 'can't keep her hands off'n me. I suppose it's understandable. With my charm and looks, she sez I'm the perfect frigging gentlemen.'

'And the perfect frigging fool, as well,' Matz intoned mournfully. 'I've seen the big bastard look at yer. If looks could kill—'

'You worry too much, Matzi,' Schulze cut him off. 'Thinking too much and too much of the old five-fingered widow.' He guffawed at the look on his friend's face and made an obscene gesture with his clenched right hand. 'You ought to get yerself a nice juicy bedmate like me.'

But Matz didn't rise to the bait. His mind was too full of forebodings . . .

On the morning of the third day, Colonel Sturmer assembled his battalion with Greul and von Dodenburg flanking him. Waiting till they stamped the new snow off their boots and took their places on the floor of the barracks gym, Sturmer eyed his men. He liked what he saw; even the new recruits, mostly from the Bavarian alpine region, were bronzed, fit and hard. After all they had absorbed the lore of the mountains with their mother's milk. Still, something told him a lot of them would not be coming back to their beloved mountains; so far everything was proceeding too easily. And he didn't like operations that started so well. They always ended in trouble.

'*Morgen, Soldaten*!' he called when they were finally seated.

'*Morgen, Herr Oberst*,' the reply came back from five hundred confident young voices.

While Sturmer commenced his briefing, Greul slipped behind him and removed the blanket from a map. He stood there like some grim-faced guardian of the great secret, as if daring anyone to approach more closely, his arms folded across his chest.

'Here is Mount Elbrus,' Sturmer explained, 'the highest peak. Over five thousand metres high. We have been given the mission of climbing it. Not for any military reason, but for the greater glory of our National Socialist Germany.'

Von Dodenburg frowned at the Colonel's irony; it was not the kind of talk one expected from a senior *Wehrmacht* officer. But it was wasted on the mass of his listeners. They burst into an excited buzz of chatter at the disclosure. As for the fervent Nazi, Greul, he seemed to grow in stature, his face very proud, as if he had personally achieved something of importance.

Sturmer raised his hand to stop the chatter and continued, 'Now, men, you must not think this is going to be a pleasurable jaunt – a time out of war. It isn't.' He tapped the map again. 'Before we can reach even the foothills around Elbrus, we will have to pass through sixty kilometres of enemy-held territory. As far as Intelligence knows, the Red Army has evacuated the area and retreated deeper into the Caucasus mountains. But there are still partisans to be reckoned with, lost Red Army battalions and the like.' He paused momentarily. '*And*, according again to Intelligence, the men of the Karatski tribe with their main base at the village of Chursuk – *here*.'

He paused and let his words sink in. Von Dodenburg saw for the first time what Wotan's light armour was going to be used for. His men and tanks were going to provide protection for the lightly armed mountaineers. Protection they would need until they reached the base of the mountain and commenced their climb. He frowned. He didn't like the idea one bit. Armour in mountains was always a decidedly risky business. The tanks' cannon would be of little use against partisans and the like. And tanks would be very vulnerable to determined foot soldiers, even if they were only armed with grenades and home-made Molotov cocktails.[*]

'Now these Karatski tribesmen are by tradition bandits – and Muslims. In theory they are against the Reds, who don't believe in religion. But that doesn't mean' – Sturmer stared hard at his young soldiers, as if suddenly needing to etch their earnest, eager young faces on his mind's eye – 'that they are automatically on our side. We can, therefore, regard them as potential enemies, very cunning ones too – and cruel. According to Intelligence they have some pretty unpleasant methods for dealing with anyone they care to take prisoner.'

It was too much for Schulze, sitting just in front of von Dodenburg, along with Matz. He simpered in what he supposed was a female falsetto, 'Don't tell me they'll make me a singing tenor if they get their evil paws on me, sir.' He clutched the front of his trousers to make his meaning quite clear.

'Yes, Sergeant Schulze, I suppose it could mean something like that,' Sturmer said with a faint smile on his lips, while Ox-Jo frowned and clenched his fist threateningly. 'But don't worry Sergeant. The way you fellers of the SS go at it, it'll be bound to drop off of its own accord in due course.'

Schulze's remark had defused the situation a little. Sturmer was glad of it for he guessed his mountaineers had now realized what they had let themselves in for and weren't too happy with the thought. He cleared his throat and continued, 'Providing we don't have any trouble with these tribesmen

[*] A glass jar filled with petrol and ignited by a fuse, which could at close range set an armoured vehicle alight. *Transl.*

36

who worry Sergeant Schulze here, we'll pass through Chursuk and head for the Choryu pass – here. It's about three thousand metres above sea level and the met people guess there'll be snow up there.' He looked at von Dodenburg. 'If there is, that is where we and your Wotan will part company, *Hauptsturmbannführer.*'

Von Dodenburg nodded his understanding, but said nothing.

'However, if everything goes as planned, we should reach Elbrus House – here.' Sturmer tapped the map once more. 'By the end of our first day of marching.'

'Elbrus House?' It was Ox-Jo, obviously wanting to show that he was a person of some importance: one who dare interrupt the CO and ask questions 'What's that, sir?'

'I've seen a photo of it, Sergeant Mayr, and there's not much else I can tell you about it. Apparently the Popovs built it before the war. It is supposed to be covered with some sort of alloy, perhaps aluminium. That should make it proof against all types of weather; deep frost, hot, baking sun and the like. It was intended to be a weather station, but whether the Popovs managed to complete it before the war is not known,' said Sturmer. 'At any event, Sergeant Mayr, and the rest of you, we shall rest there a day and prepare for the ascent of the West Peak.' Sturmer nodded to Greul. Hastily the Major produced an illuminated picture of the peak and von Dodenburg gave a little shudder at his first sight of the West Peak of Elbrus. It was a sheer wall of white; harsh and cruel, silhouetted against the background of a hard blue sky. There was something remote and frightening about the peak. Before the war, when von Dodenburg had been stationed at Berchtesgaden as Himmler's adjutant, he had gone climbing in the local mountains, even tackling the Watzmann[*] on his own. But he had never liked climbing and as he viewed that cruel peak, he felt even less anxious to do so. Climbing mountains, he told himself, needed a special kind of temperament: that of the loner who challenged nature, knowing right from the start that that challenge might well end in his own death. He shuddered slightly at the thought.

---

[*]Germany's second highest mountain. *Transl.*

As usual Sergeant Schulze was ready with one of his bawdy quips, totally unmoved by that fearsome peak. As Sturmer added, 'the West Peak is the real peak, but the other peak you can see on the photo, men, is one hundred metres lower', he called, 'Looks to me like a pair of tits, sir. Perhaps we should call it Twin-Tit Mountain. Look good in the headlines, sir, once you've climbed the thing. German Mountaineers Plant the Swastika Flag on Left Nipple of Twin-Tit Mountain!'

'*Sergeant Schulze.*' Geier cried in outrage, his face flushed a furious red. 'How dare you speak like that . . . You are insulting our glorious flag.'

Sturmer held up his hand for silence while some of the younger men laughed softly, both at what Schulze thought was his brilliant humour and at Major Greul's enraged discomfort. '*Schon gut*, Schulze,' he said, 'that's enough of that. Please, Major Greul, would you have the kindness to let me finish?' Without waiting to see if Greul would, he went on with, 'At Elbrus House I shall personally select the best of the climbers to complete the ascent. With the weather on our side, I feel we can do so and be down again in twenty-four hours, though the ascent will be a matter of trial and error. Intelligence has been unable to turn up any Popov material on the difficulty of the climb and as far as our people in the west are concerned, no one seems to have tackled the final bit since before the Russian revolution.' He allowed himself a brief smile. 'No matter, if anyone can do it, it is you, comrades.'

His words were greeted with a cheer and his smile broadened but vanished abruptly as if he had suddenly had an unpleasant thought. 'But remember this.' He looked at the smiling faces of his mountaineers earnestly. 'Although this is almost a peacetime operation, we are still at war with the Popovs, who might not be there, but then again they might. All of us must keep one eye on the summit of Elbrus Mountain. At the same time however, we must keep our other one to our rear – just in case some nasty Popov partisan or the like is about to shaft us with something particularly unpleasant . . . Any questions?' He fumbled in the upper pocket of his tunic for a cigarette and relaxed, pretending not to see the look of shocked horror on Greul's face as he puffed out smoke – for the tall Major this was a heinous crime.

But no questions came. For all of them, even the usually irrepressible Schulze, were silent, each man shrouded in his own thoughts and apprehensions. Sturmer stubbed out the cigarette after a couple more puffs at it and raising his voice said, '*Kameraden*, we are finished with our preparations. Tomorrow, before first light, we roll at zero six hundred hours. But tonight we celebrate. Who knows?' he shrugged but didn't finish the words. Instead he said. 'Beer, sausage and schnapps will be paid for by the battalion funds. *Hoch die Tassen, Kameraden . . . die Nacht wird kuhl*.*' And even before Sergeant Ox-Jo Mayr could call the room to attention, the colonel had touched his hand to his cap in a kind of a salute and had vanished into the crowd of men.

Behind him, Matz commented, 'Decent fellah that – for an officer. Free suds and firewater, my, my, my. What a night it's gonna be.'

His running mate, Schulze, obviously was not as concerned with the free suds and firewater. He had other things on his evil mind. He whispered, 'And tonight, old house, I'm gonna get young Hannelore's drawers down if it's the last thing I do.'

A few metres away stood Ox-Jo. If he had known of Schulze's intentions at that moment, he might well have commented in his thick Bavarian growling voice, 'And if you try, *Saupreuss*, it is gonna be the last thing you do . . .'

---

*A soldiers' toast: literally 'Up the cups, the night's gonna be cold'. *Transl.*

Seven

'*Kameraden*,' Ox-Jo bellowed above the noisy racket of the smoke-filled mess hall. 'In a minute the piss-up will commence but I'd like to say a few words to you cardboard soldiers.'

His words were received by boos and wet kisses from the crowded tables, where the young men eyed the crates of Munich beer set up at regular intervals along the scrubbed wooden tables. 'Give it a rest', a young man bolder than the rest called, 'Let's get down to the serious stuff of supping suds.'

After a suitable amount of time had passed, Sturmer, standing with Greul at the back of the big room, already heavy with the smell of pig's knuckle, *sauerkraut* and mashed potatoes being prepared in the battalion kitchens beyond, gave the major a nudge. 'Greul,' he whispered, 'I think we'd better give it a rest, too. They'll feel more at ease without the officers' presence.'

Greul pulled a face. 'In truth, sir,' he answered. 'I can't get out of this place soon enough. Look at that man over there, sir. The one being sick – and he's smoking too. Bah!'

Sturmer grinned. One of the young recruits was already vomiting into a steel helmet at his side. If that wasn't enough, some wag had placed a smoking cigarette in his right ear so that every time he retched miserably, smoke puffed out of his left one.' Young men, full of piss and vinegar, Greul,' he said carelessly, as if that explained everything. 'Come on, let's go quietly.'

Ox-Jo was laying down the ground rules for their last *kameradschaftsabend** in Bad Reichenhall before the troops

---

*Literally 'comradeship's evening', a kind of company smoker. *Transl.*

set off on their mission. 'There'll be no pissing in the hall, anyone who eats too much *sauerkraut* and starts farting will get a taste of my boot.'

Schulze said to Matz, 'I should think the coast is clear now. By the time that big Bavarian bastard has filled his guts and sunk a couple of litres of beer, I'll have had it.'

Matz looked worried. 'You're chancing it, Schulzi,' he whispered back. 'Yer can't trust them hairy-arsed peasants from the mountains. Too much inbreeding. Most of them are half crazy. If he finds out you've been dicking his girl—' But Schulze was already sliding along the wall to the exit, avoiding the recruit hanging from the hatstand by his collar, totally out of this world.

Hannelore was in her little room at the end of the kitchen. She was bent over the gleaming rings of *Knackwurst* and *Weisswurst*, the Bavarian favourite, routinely cutting up two of each type of sausage and passing them through the little window where the sweating kitchen bulls waited to boil them and add them to the steaming plates of mashed potato and *sauerkraut* waiting to be served to the soldiers.

The big blonde was so caught up in her work, her lips moving silently as she counted off the fours, that she had not noticed that her tight skirt had ridden up at the back to reveal a tantalizing stretch of delightful black silk leg. Sergeant Schulze had however. He licked his lips as if they were suddenly very dry and muttered, 'lovely grub'.

He couldn't help himself. He shot both of his big hands forward and before Hannelore realized he was there, he had thrust them high under her skirt.

Hannelore jumped and nearly sliced her fingers off instead of the sausage. She gave a little yelp and turned round, her face flushed and angry. 'Why you dirty swine, Sergeant Mayr. Have you no shame—' The indignant words died on her lips as she saw who it was. Almost immediately her face was transformed. 'Sergeant Schulze, it's *you*!' She beamed at him. 'Would you like me to boil you a couple of sausages away from that rough crowd in there?'

Schulze shook his head, and put what he imagined a look of true love looked like on his broad, homely face, 'It is not

41

food I desire, my beloved,' he declared gallantly. He blew her a kiss and her face was wreathed in a cloud of garlic-laden breath. 'It is *you*.'

Hannelore ignored the garlic, if she even noticed it; she was so entranced by the charm of Frau Schulze's handsome son, as he always described himself in his modest fashion. 'What beautiful things you say – *Hans*. May I call you that?'

'*Naturlich mein Schatz*. But let's not waste time.'

The big blonde knew exactly what Schulze meant. Indeed the big bulge at the front of his trousers was all the indication she needed to judge Schulze's intentions; and as eager as she was, those intentions worried her. 'But if *he* finds out—' she began.

'Nothing shall come between true love, my little darling,' Schulze interrupted her passionately and placed his big hands on her breasts, which were threatening to overflow from the low-cut blouse she was wearing. She shuddered.

'Oh,' she moaned, her eyes turning upwards, as if she was in the throes of an unbearable passion. 'Oh Please . . . Please – give it to me!'

He clapped one hand across her mouth to quieten her. 'Lower my darling,' he ordered, 'or you'll have the lot of them getting the hots.'

Recklessly she thrust his hand away and pressed her nubile body against his, savouring the hardness of his loins, 'I don't care, Hans . . . I'll do anything, anything you want.' Blindly she proceeded to do so, feeling for his flies, grabbing open each button until she could pull out that which she desired, cooing, 'Oh, God in Heaven. Are . . . are you going to put *that* . . . enormous thing inside of poor little me?'

'You betcha!' Schulze said enthusiastically, as he nuzzled the front of her knickers with its head.

'Then do it – *now*!' she commanded in a harsh strained voice he hardly recognized.

'But you've got your knickers on – your best ones.'

'Then rip them off this very instant,' she ordered. For a moment, Sergeant Schulze, the man who always boasted he'd had more beaver than other men had had hot dinners, was afraid. How could she be so demanding?

Outside, the band of the civilian *Schutzenverein*, all booming drums and blaring brass, struck up the 'Bavarian Parade March'. Thus to the regular thump, thump of the ancient drummer's big drum, Hannelore and Hans consummated their great love on the kitchen table among the slimy lengths of *Weisswurst*, Ox-Jo's favourite delicacy . . .

Ox-Jo was drunk, very drunk. Still as he held onto the wall outside, aiming unsteady streams of steaming yellow urine at the grate, he recognized the couple immediately and even in his state he didn't need a crystal ball to help him understand what had been going on.

Hannelore, his girl, and that big Prussian swine had been at it – indeed if his eyes didn't deceive him, the two of them were *still* at it. '*Sakrament,*' he cursed, in the Bavarian fashion, and was so shocked that he missed the grate and urinated all over his best pair of mountain boots. 'The *Saupreuss* has got his hand up her skirt.'

In truth, Schulze, as shaken as he was at having Hannelore jumping up and down on him only five minutes before, had got his hand up more than the delighted blonde's skirt, while she was tugging in and out at his penis as if it was a length of rubber hose.

What exactly they were up to didn't concern Ox-Jo at that moment. What concerned him was a burning desire to have his revenge on the man who had obviously raped Hannelore. With his penis, empty now of urine, still dangling out of his open flies, he grabbed his jack-knife that all Bavarians worthy of their salt carried in their back pockets. With a flick of his big thumbnail, he opened it, the blade gleaming an evil silver in the light of the half-moon. 'Bastard,' he roared in wild fury and charged forward.

'Hans!' the blonde screamed.

Schulze swung round, his erection vanishing in a flash. He saw the drunk giant rushing at him at once. 'Holy mackerel,' he cried. 'The bugger's *meschugge*. He's got a knife—'

In that same instant, Ox-Jo lunged at him wildly. But the beer had made him just a little too slow. Schulze sprang to one side and as he did, he thrust out his foot. Ox-Jo staggered but managed to stay on his feet. Schulze kicked him

43

hard and he staggered another few paces. Still he didn't fall – and he kept hold of his knife.

'Give me your cape,' Schulze commanded urgently. '*Schnell, Madchen!*'

She flung the cape, made of thick green *loden* cloth, at Schulze. The latter caught it in one hand just as Ox-Jo prepared to charge again, knife held tightly to his hip. Hastily, Schulze wrapped the cape round his left arm. He was just in time. Ox-Jo lunged. Schulze grunted with pain as the blade penetrated his arm through the thick cloth of the cape.

Ox-Jo, carried away by the momentum of his wild rush, slammed into Schulze and nearly knocked him over – but not quite. Schulze didn't hesitate. He brought up his right knee viciously and stuck it into Ox-Jo's groin.

Ox-Jo gagged. For a second, Schulze thought he was going to be sick all over him. He hung in there, weird noises coming from deep down in his big body, his hands holding on to his injured testicles. Then with sheer, naked will-power, he pulled himself erect and aimed another blow at Schulze. But the latter had had enough. His fist slammed down hard on the Bavarian's shoulder. He yelped with pain. The knife tumbled from his hand to the cobbles of the path. Schulze didn't give him a chance to pick it up. As the Bavarian attemped to do so, Schulze brought up his knee sharply. It connected with the point of the Bavarian's big chin. He gave a muffled groan and sank to his knees, like a boxer refusing to go down for a count of ten. But Schulze showed no mercy. As a moaning Ox-Jo knelt there, Schulze hit him hard in the face. The SS NCO felt his fist suddenly wet with something warm, the blood from Ox-Jo's broken nose. In the next instant, Ox-Jo flopped on to the cobbles beaten and out to the world.

Inside the dining room, the drunken troops stamped their feet as the band played on. Men were being sick everywhere. A corporal, stark naked, was running around shouting, 'Catch me, I'm the spring'. For what reason no one knew or cared. In the kitchen, the female auxiliaries had fearfully barricaded themselves in, each woman armed with a cleaver or the heavy wooden tool they used for mashing potatoes. They were Bavarians themselves, they knew to what length these rough mountain boys would go when they were in their cups. And the men were getting out of hand. They'd be trying to break the kitchen door down soon to enjoy what they called harmlessly in dialect a '*gaudi*'*, but which really amounted to rape. The frightened peasant women were mistaken. For just then, for some reason known only to themselves, the drunken cry went up, 'Where's Sergeant Mayr . . . where's good old Ox-Jo?' Not that Ox-Jo was a popular man but the men knew he was the wildest of them all. If anything was going to happen with women that night, Ox-Jo was sure to be the instigator.

'He's outside having a piss.' someone cried out crazily.

'No,' another objected, 'he's dancing the mattress polka with that big Hannelore of his. Outside, he's bound to be out there somewhere . . .'

'*Outside!*' fifty drunken voices took up the cry and they staggered and stumbled towards the door, skidding in the pools of vomit, falling over the 'beer corpses' of their comrades, lying on the floor out of the world, out into the freezing cold of the starlit mountain night and stopped dead at the sight which met them there.

---

*Bavarian dialect, roughly meaning 'fun'. *Transl.*

Eight

Colonel Sturmer was still awake when his concentration was disturbed by the racket coming from the barracks square. For a while he didn't let it worry him; he was too concerned with the latest sparse information that Intelligence had sent him about Mount Elbrus. Apparently, the stainless-steel house, some three thousand metres up the side of the great mountain, was some sort of hotel that had been constructed back in the late thirties. As he looked at the poor quality pre-war photograph of the place, noting automatically that it could be easily defended by a handful of men and enjoyed an excellent field-of-fire, he worried about whether it was occupied. If it was it would be necessary to take the place, before his men could commence the final ascent on the peak, and that would take time and men.

Slowly the noise from outside started to penetrate his consciousness. At first he told himself that it was probably the usual noisiness of the troops celebrating the *Kameradschaftsaben* before the sergeant-of-the-guard began threatening them to go back to their barracks; it was almost time for 'lights out'. But the noise continued and he couldn't hear the usual harsh commands, curses and threats of the guard commander. He frowned and in the end gave in. He had better go and see what was happening. Cursing a little to himself, he grabbed his cap and greatcoat and left his quarters.

He didn't get far. Fifty metres away, illuminated by the silver light of the cold stars, he saw what was happening and stopped short, hardly daring to believe his own eyes.

In the centre of a mob of howling, drunken mountaineers, the three SS men stood backed against the wall, the arro

46

gant young *Hauptsturmbannführer*, von Dodenburg, with his pistol drawn and ready to fire at his men. Some metres away, a hesitant sergeant-of-the-guard, carbine slung over his shoulder, stood over the unconscious body of a mountain NCO, whom he recognized as Ox-Jo Mayr.

What had happened he didn't know. What he did know instantly was that there was serious trouble brewing. He had to act immediately, or God knows what might happen. He cupped his hands above his mouth and yelled, 'Sergeant!'

'Sir?'

'Turn out the guard.'

The sergeant didn't react. It was almost as if he were more scared of the mob than the CO.

'*Sergeant*,' Sturmer bellowed again. 'Do you hear me?'

This time Sturmer's cry was so loud that, even surrounded by the yelling mob, von Dodenburg, Schulze and Matz also heard him. Von Dodenburg gritted his teeth, but loosened the grip on his pistol trigger a little. Even so, he kept staring in his most threatening manner at those of the drunken mountaineers to his left and right who were most likely to rush him if he lowered his guard.

Behind him, Schulze waved his ceremonial NCO's short bayonet and chortled, still a little drunk. 'Come on, you Bavarian barn-shitters, I'll carve your rotten Bavarian balls off yer, with pleasure.' He made a cutting movement with the bayonet to indicate exactly what he had in mind for the mob that was pushing forward, preparing to rush the three SS men.

'Hold yer trap,' Matz warned but his warning went unheeded. He knew that neither Schulze's defiant stance nor the rage of the CO would save them if the angered mountaineers rushed them, which they would do in half a moment.

Von Dodenburg had faced up to rebellious soldiers before. Last winter, in the great *Wehrmacht* retreat from Moscow, he had stood up to men more than once, had been prepared to use his weapon against soldiers who had broken line and were attempting to flee to the rear. But that had been in Russia, with a whole army disintegrating under tremendous pressure. This was different, he was in Germany facing a lot

47

of drunken, foolish young men – a lot of them new recruits. A corporal to his right started to move. He was armed with a beer bottle, raised above his head threateningly like a club. 'Stop there,' von Dodenburg commanded sternly and jerked up the muzzle of his pistol.

'Piss in the wind, sow-Prussian!' the corporal growled drunkenly. 'All right, boys, what are you waiting for? There's only three of the bastards. *Los—*'

The rest of the corporal's words were drowned as Sturmer, seizing the petrified guard-sergeant's rifle, fired three sharp shots into the sky, crying, 'The next bullet is aimed at you, Corporal Brettlmayr!'

The corporal with the bottle stopped dead.

'Now drop that bottle . . . Don't waste my time . . .' Sturmer was harsh and angry as he levelled his rifle at the NCO. '*NOW*!'

The NCO shook his head, as if he were waking from a bad dream. The next instant he let the bottle drop. It shattered on the cobbles. His action seemed to act as some kind of signal for the rest of the men. The tension relaxed immediately, their shoulders slumped, their bodies looked suddenly deflated, like a balloon after the air was let out. Suddenly the sergeant-of-the-guard came out of his trance-like state. His voice low and apologetic, he asked, 'Can I have my rifle back, sir? Sorry sir . . . Don't know what came over me. All right, you lot, get back to your billets.'

Major Greul appeared. He was naked, despite the freezing cold, save for his boots and shorts but, as always, Greul believed in absolute physical hardness. He took in the situation at once as he saw the crestfallen, ashamed troops being herded back to their barracks, all fight vanished. Hands placed contemptuously on his hips, he raged, 'The elite of the German mountain troops, eh. What scum you really are in truth . . . a drunken mob. If I had my way, I'd shoot every tenth man of you . . . For God's sake, sergeant-of-the-guard, get them out of my sight before I lose my temper with them.'

Watching him, Sturmer shook his head slightly, as if he couldn't comprehend the world anymore, before turning to a pale-faced von Dodenburg. 'Well?' he said.

Von Dodenburg, thrusting his pistol back into his holster, didn't react. He didn't know whether the 'well' indicated a question which he was supposed to answer. If it did, he didn't have an answer to the events of the last few minutes. Von Dodenburg said tonelessly to Matz and Schulze, both very subdued, 'Get back to your quarters. Pack your gear. We're taking the early morning train from Bad Reichenhall to Munich. The sooner we're out of here the better.'

'Sir.' They clicked to attention and saluted. Wordlessly they turned and walked away – even Schulze, with his big mouth, had nothing more to say.

Sturmer waited till they were out of earshot before saying softly, almost as if talking to himself, 'Not a very good start, eh? I mean between your Wotan and my mountaineers.'

'No sir,' von Dodenburg agreed. He opened his heart to the tall lean colonel, 'I am not very happy about this mission as it is, sir. Of course, the Führer, in his wisdom, knows what he is doing. Yet I still feel it is not right to risk the lives of your and my men in his mission, which is essentially a peace time mission, one of prestige, with no military value.'

Sturmer nodded, but didn't say anything for a long while, or so it seemed to von Dodenburg. The barracks was settling down again; there was no sound now save for the steady stamp of the sentries' boots on the gravel of the perimeter and the hush of night wind in the skeletal trees. In the end, however, he broke his silence and said, 'I shall not see you for a while, von Dodenburg, but remember this; although we might belong to different camps, we shall work together, *not* for the glory of the Third Reich –' Even as Sturmer said the words, von Dodenburg realized that the mountaineer was taking a great risk talking to him like this. After all he was an officer in the SS – 'but to ensure our men survive. There's where our duty lies, von Dodenburg. To look after our young men, come what may.' He thrust out his hand. 'Good luck, von Dodenburg, till we meet again. 'With that he turned and strode away and was swallowed up by the shadows at the edge of the barracks square.

While the three SS men packed in silence, knowing that

it would be better that they cleared the mountaineers' barracks before Sturmer's troopers set off on their long journey to the Caucasus, Sturmer decided it was no use attempting to sleep now. His mind was too full. He thought of what was to come and, after tonight's events, he thought things would not go as smoothly as expected. There were too many imponderables involved.

The English, the fat members of the nineteenth century bourgeoise, had started the sport of climbing as a means of escape from the commercialism of Victorian city life. What had the early English climber, Edward Whymper, called it – climbing as a new dimension of existence?

On the one hand, the Tommies had wanted to escape from civilisation – the man-made disaster of Victorian England, with its smoke-belching factories and the stunted, underfed operatives. But on the other, they saw climbing as a symbol that human beings could tame nature; that the puny creatures that they were could conquer the highest peaks.

He collected his kit together, laying it out neatly on his bunk, checking each item carefully as a good mountaineer should, deciding whether it was necessary and what it would weigh when it was packed in the limited space of his climbing rucksack. Sturmer considered the theory of those early English climbers, a theory which had been adopted by their Nazi successers. Nature was not something you could conquer. Nature was simply there. The idea of a conquest of a mountain didn't appeal to him, that of escape from the purposeless activity of the city and state did.

He paused and looked at himself in the mirror on the wall underneath one of the Nazi mottoes that adorned the barracks, *Ein Reich, ein Volk, ein Führer.* 'One Empire, One People, One Leader' he mused, talking to the mirror. Perhaps that was what he really detested, the reason that he wanted to escape to the mountains. He grinned at himself and tipped his hand to his head in a gesture that many would have thought was one of farewell. Suddenly, surprisingly, he said to himself – though the abrupt thought didn't seem to worry him one bit – 'I'm not coming back . . .'

PART TWO
A Journey Into the Unknown

One

It had stopped snowing as they had approached the foothills which marked the border to the Caucasus. As the slow Soviet train carried Wotan's C Company deeper into the country, toward their mission, the troopers, squatting at the doors of the open carriages or lounging on the flat cars which bore the new Skoda self-propelled guns, spotted peasants leading their animals into the lush low meadows to enjoy the new grass. Now and again they saw long caravans of camels laden with goods and mostly herded by women, who pulled up the seams of their gowns to hide their dark faces when they saw the men. This caused Schulze to grab the front of his trousers and comment, without too much enthusiasm,' I could make their eyes pop with what I've got here, comrades!'

To which Matz replied, 'Eyes pop. If their menfolk caught hold of yer, Schulzi, it wouldn't just be yer eyes that would pop. They're very fussy about who they let look at their women.'

But despite the constant threat, it all seemed very peaceful to the men in the little train steadily heading east. 'A time out of war,' von Dodenburg remarked to young Cadet Haas, with whom he shared the train's only real compartment. Haas, a blond eighteen-year-old who had just joined Wotan from the SS Cadet School at Bad Toelz, was inclined to agree, though the fact there was apparently no prospect of immediate action disappointed him. Like most boys of his age from Hitler Youth background, he yearned for some desperate glory so that he could return home covered with medals to be feted as a hero.

But for the time being von Dodenburg, who liked the boy,

53

seeing in him something of himself as he had been as a cadet in, what now seemed, another age, kept the cadet busy sorting out the escape kit that Himmler had personally provided for the company. As he had explained over the phone to von Dodenburg just before they had left Berlin, 'If this mission proposed by Herr Bormann goes wrong, I don't want my SS to be associated with him. The men must escape, not allow themselves to be captured.'

Von Dodenburg had smiled and agreed. Himmler, Bormann, Goering and the rest were like party chieftains, each out to gain the Führer's favour, but at the same time not daring either to risk his displeasure by failing him. So von Dodenburg kept the eager young cadet at it, allotting what Himmler had called 'the survival stores'. Escape kit would not have been the right description for the SS, who fought to the last, as the Reichsführer saw it. There were magnetic razor blades that could be turned into a compass in an emergency, pliable surgical saws, covered with textile, that could be used as shoelaces for mountain boots, rubber bottles that might hold water, fishing hooks and heaps of other gear that an escapee might need. As Sergeant Schulze had commented as he had helped the young cadet to unpack the gear, 'Fishing hooks, sir! What in three devils is this? *Are we going on a frigging fishing trip?*'

Many of the bored troopers, lolling in their open trucks, might well have hoped they were. The rank-and-file didn't yet know what their mission was; von Dodenburg had thought it better they didn't. As was customary under such circumstances, rumours, or 'latrinograms', as they called them, abounded. 'Have yer heard the latest, old house?' they would say, 'Himmler's sending us into the Caucasus to find Noah's Ark?'

'Get off it,' others would sneer in disbelief. 'We're off to India to meet up with the Nips and finish off them tea-swilling Tommies for frigging good.'

Lulled by the boredom of the long journey, the troop's train lookouts started to become careless, fighting to keep their eyes open as the little train chugged eastwards at a steady thirty kilometres an hour. Their boredom was only broken by the never-ending bowls of 'fart soup', as they called the daily ration of pea soup, or cups of weak ersatz coffee; their minds and imagination preocuppied – as it always is with bored young men – with lascivious thoughts of nubile young women.

Von Dodenburg was lecturing young Haas on the tribes of the lower part of the Caucasus. 'They're on the whole anti-Russian – after all, they've only been part of the former Russian Empire since the late nineteenth century – but that doesn't mean they're pro-German. They're simply out for themselves.' At this point they had their first alarm since they had set out on their mission. It came in the form of riders on the heights, who kept up with the train as it slogged its way up a steep incline, belching smoke. The jingling of the pebble-filled tin, which von Dodenburg had rigged up in the officers' compartment, was suddenly heard.

It was a primitive device, commonly used on troop trains in Russia, a kind of bush telegraph. It was linked to the driver's cab on the locomotive, and when the driver pulled the string attaching it to the front of the train, it warned the train commander that there was trouble of some sort up ahead.

The next moment, the train, ascending a steep rise leading up to a pass, where von Dodenburg knew a small Caucasian village and whistle-stop primitive station were located, started to slow even more. Von Dodenburg acted immediately; he knew that speedy, decisive action was usually needed at such moments. 'Haas,' he snapped urgently, 'get your weapon.'

Haas's face lit up excitedly. 'Action, sir?' he asked eagerly.

Von Dodenburg didn't answer. He had other, more important things to do. Leaning dangerously out of the door of the compartment, he yelled at Matz squatting at the door of his own box car, 'Corporal Matz, what do you make of them?'

Matz, who had the keenest sense of smell and the best eyesight of the whole company, reacted immediately. He knew, without further explanation, what the CO expected of him. He turned in the direction of the riders. His nose twitched like some anxious mountain goat of his native Bavaria, scenting trouble, while von Dodenburg waited anxiously. A moment later, his answer came. 'Popovs, sir. You can smell that mahorka of theirs kilometres off. The stuff stinks to high heaven.' He meant the coarse black tobacco the Russians smoked which came wrapped in pieces of newspaper torn from the *Ivestia* or *Pravda* and the like. 'And there's an officer with them.'

Haas, clutching his machine pistol, asked in wonder, 'How does he know that, sir?'

'These wandering rider patrols have little chance to wash, Haas. They're usually rife with lice. So the officers douse themselves with cheap scent. It's supposed to kill the vermin . . . Come on!'

Lightly, von Dodenburg dropped out of the carriage as the old train slowed down even more. Narrowing his eyes against the thick black wood smoke coming from the locomotive, von Dodenburg could see what had caused their Russian volunteer driver, Grigor, to sound the alarm. Up ahead, where the track disappeared over the narrow pass, someone had piled up logs and chopped down telegraph poles and supported the heap with large boulders. It was obvious what was going on. 'They're trying to derail us, Haas,' von Dodenburg shouted at the excited cadet, who was running after him, brandishing his Schmeisser. 'Come on!'

'But who . . .?' Haas's question died on his lips. The CO was not listening. Instead he was pelting towards the tender where the fireman, another Russian volunteer, was gripping his rifle with blackened hands, while the driver looked through the aperture. Hands on the controls, he stared grimly at the barricade ahead.

'What do you think, Grigor?' von Dodenburg gasped.

'Don't know,' the driver said in good German. 'Regulations say—'

'Damn the regulations,' von Dodenburg said, cutting the ethnic German short. As always these ethnic minorities, who were former Russian citizens, were more German than the Germans. 'If we stop up there, the Ivans'll start picking us off like flies. Keep on going, but slow.'

As if to lend weight to his words there was a slow chatter of a Russian machine gun fire from a clump of stunted olive

56

trees to their right. A series of bright steel holes was ripped the length of the tender. The fireman yelped with pain and reeled back, blood pouring from a wound on his forehead.

Carried away by his first taste of combat, Haas raised his machine pistol and loosed off a wild burst in the direction of the trees A Russian tumbled down the slope, sliding into a stream of loose stones. In the next instant a horse bolted out of olive trees, galloping off riderless. The machine gun fire intensified.

That burst of fire seemed to act as a signal for the Wotan troopers. Leaning out of the doors of their box cars, or firing through the gaps in the slitted wooden walls, they started to return fire, with Schulze crying, 'Come on, you dogs, you don't want to live for ever, do you?' But the Wotan troopers didn't need any encouragement from the big NCO. All of them, even the newest recruit, knew what would happen to them if they fell into the hands of what they guessed were the Cossack riders. They'd die all right but slowly, very slowly.

The locomotive was crawling along at barely five kilometres an hour, with the Volga German driver, Grigor, watching his controls and the way ahead like a hawk. He had his own plan. If he could manage to get close enough to the barricade without the enemy rupturing the locomotive's boiler with their fire, he'd apply the brakes. Thus he would slide the train into the heap of logs and boulders, instead of hitting it full tilt. With luck he'd push the barricade to one side and continue without derailing the train. It was going to be a damned difficult manoeuvre, but it was the only one he could think of. Grigor knew that if *he* fell into Russian hands, his death would be worse than that of the SS men. 'Hold on,' Grigor cried, above the angry snap-and-crackle of small arms fire. 'The bitch'll either do it or she'll frigging well bust in the attempt!'

Von Dodenburg grinned momentarily at the driver's sudden outburst. Next to him, the cadet sprayed bursts of fire to his left and right, while von Dodenburg held his own. He might need a full magazine of slugs in a moment or two.

As they came closer the Russian's hand grabbed the brake

lever; smoke poured from the boiler, slugs howled off the cab like tropical raindrops off a tin roof. Any minute now the driver would have to break and then . . . von Dodenburg didn't dare think that particular thought to its end.

'*Now!*' Grigor pulled the brake. At the same time he dropped the sand which would help him brake. The wheels clattered furiously; there was the stink of stressed steel, smoke poured back into the cab making them cough and choke. The cadet stumbled and nearly dropped his Schmeisser.

Then the engine crashed full tilt into the barricade. Logs flew through the air. Von Dodenburg yelled. A rock smashed into the side of the locomotive. The engine shook. For one horrifying second the soldiers thought the old train was going to overturn. It didn't. And an instant later they were through the barricade sliding along the track with a great ear-splitting howl, scattering broken logs to left and right.

A shaken Grigor released the brake. The train's speed started to increase – for a while. Hastily, von Dodenburg handed the shaken driver his bottle of fiery pepper vodka, which he kept in the cab. He took a great gulp of it, straight from the neck of the bottle.

Behind them, the sound of firing began to die away and then, except for a few scattered shots, ended altogether. On the heights, the riders, probably Red Army Cossacks, vanished too. All was silent, save the steady rumble of the train's wheels and, unknown to the relieved Wotan troopers, the drip-drip of the water leaking from beneath the loco-motive. It was coming straight from the boiler. The Russian bullets had penetrated the thinner steel there. Slowly, but surely, the gauge which indicated the water pressure started to slip to the left. Company C, SS Assault Regiment Wotan was in trouble.

Two

While the troopers, under Haas's command, unloaded one of the smaller troop carriers from the flat cars, von Dodenburg stared in a mixture of anger and frustration at the locomotive. It still puffed steam like a weary old warrior that was going to give up the ghost but attempted to keep going valiantly, but it was clear, even without Grigor's explanation, that it was unable to pull the troop train and its heavy load of men and vehicles.

Von Dodenburg rubbed his unshaven jaw and stared at the sun; a dull-red ball above the snow-tipped peaks of the far mountains. He guessed it would remain there for about an hour or so before it vanished and they would be left in the middle of nowhere, save for the whistle-stop somewhere to the front. They would be vulnerable to attack. 'Grigor,' he broke the heavy silence. 'What's the drill when this sort of thing happens?'

The driver, who was well into his bottle of pepper vodka, growled, 'It shouldn't happen.'

'But if it does?' von Dodenburg humoured him. 'I'm sure there is some kind of system?'

The Volka German took a careful swing of the fiery liquid, for he was rationing himself, and said, 'Of course, we Germans always have a system. If we don't arrive at the next stop, the main office of the *Reichsbahn* at Maikop reports that we are overdue. They then check along their sub-section of the line to estimate where signals last saw us. When Maikop has decided where that is, our brave Italian allies, the Macaronis, sally forth to rescue us. Unfortunately, the Macaronis develop sudden deafness, especially at night and then that's that.'

'But in theory a rescue party is sent out.'

Grigor sniffed with contempt. 'In theory,' he conceded. 'But I wouldn't bank on it.'

Grigor's final words made up von Dodenburg's mind for him. It was clear that Company C would have to help itself, and to do that he needed to secure some sort of fire base at the yet unseen whistle-stop ahead. If they could get the stalled train safely through the night, he reasoned either their Italian allies who garrisoned this area could come to their assistance on the morrow or they might even be able to help themselves with whatever railway staff they might find at the whistle-stop. In all events the most important thing to do was to get Company C through the night; and that meant not letting any enemy get close enough to the train so his troops were unable to use the considerable fire-power of their Skoda self-propelled guns, still anchored to the flat cars.

His mind made up, he cupped his hands around his mouth and he yelled to Haas, 'All right, Cadet Haas, *Carbide!*'

Haas looked puzzled.

Schulze and Matz, who were going with him, plus another six volunteers, cried in unison, glad to be moving, even if it was into the unknown, 'Give gas, cadet. That's what we always say in Wotan.'

Haas, still regarding the whole business as a great adventure, grinned and echoed the yell, adding, 'Then *carbide* it is.'

They were quickly on their way, with a worried von Dodenburg automatically noting the flash of reflecting glass on the hillside to their left,

He bit his bottom lip. He knew what it signified, the Cossacks hadn't gone yet. They were still watching the train – and waiting. Grigor chanced another sip of his precious vodka, saying as if to himself, 'Here's to a frigging short life.'

Von Dodenburg was tempted to retort, 'And here's amen to that Grigor.' He caught himself in time and stayed silent.

The whistle-stop turned out to be larger than the crew had been told to expect. It was a small village in fact, made up of shabby once-white painted cottages, lining both sides of the track, with tall yellow sunflowers already reaching up to the straw-thatched roofs; and, as usual in southern Russia, where there was no electricity and the natives had to bed close to their chickens, the single street was quite busy with locals.

The Wotan troopers, who had never been in the Caucasus before, noted immediately how different the natives looked from the northern Russians they had encountered before. Northern Russians were often stocky, with pudding faces and corn-yellow hair. These locals were tall, skinny and very dark; the men wearing heavy black moustaches, the women in long gowns that reached their ankles, and half-inclined to pull their head scarves down, hiding their faces whenever they thought the newcomers were looking at them.

Yet the silky scarves and the long dresses could not hide their splendid looks. Schulze, for one, felt his blood race a little faster when his eyes lighted on one of the dark-eyed beauties, whose look seemed a mixture of rejection and, at the same time, sexual attraction. Even Matz, not normally very demonstrative, hissed at the sight of one of them, 'By the holy saint of Buxtehude, where the dogs piss through their ribs, I'd give my right testicle to put my head between her milk factories and know no pain for the rest of my natural days.'

'Stop that kind of talk, corporal,' Cadet Haas ordered, overhearing the comment, 'you know we are not supposed to fraternize with the native women.'

'*Fraternize*,' Schulze snorted, 'I don't want to *fraternize* with 'em. I want to *fuck* 'em, cadet.'

Haas blushed.

Five minutes later, Schulze and Matz squatted in the square of the little village, surrounded by curious, barefoot children, while Haas and the rest went off to trace the tumbledown clapboard station. It was their task to keep in radio touch with the stalled train round the bend and 'dominate', as Haas put it, the surrounding area. Instead, they were drinking the local sour mare's milk called *Airan*, which Matz described as being like 'a mixture of pig sweat and something that smelled of cowdung'. Not that they minded. They were thirsty and the locals, being Muslims, wouldn't have any alcohol, and they daren't touch the water. It might well be polluted and give them the thin shits, which every German soldier who served in Russia dreaded.

As it grew ever darker and there seemed no immediate danger from the Cossacks prowling somewhere in the heights above the little village, the two running mates' thoughts turned to other, more basic things than the war. As Matz finished the sour mare's milk, he pulled a face and hitched up his baggy field-grey pants purposefully. Schulze asked, 'Well?'

'Why not, old house.'

'It's hard life being a stubble-hopper,' Schulze said. 'The only things that make it worthwhile is a bit of the two-backed beast, a couple of cancer sticks and a litre of suds.'

'And we ain't got the last two,' Matz agreed. 'So, it's got to be the two-backed beast. Come on, let's go and find some good-woman –'

'*Bad's* better.'

Matz ignored the interruption – 'Who could take pity on two poor old sodgers, destined for an early grave.'

Back at the train, von Dodenburg finalized his defensive plans for the night. As the sun hesitated at the tip of the nearest snow-covered peak, he inspected his dispositions. Each self-propelled gun was manned and he had placed extra troops around the locomotive. He hoped it could be put into working order in the morning. How, he didn't know at this moment; the important thing was to get it through the night intact. As the sun finally disappeared and the steppe was abruptly bathed in darkness, he sent out a party to lay a field of 'de-ballockers' on either side of the train. These were 9mm bullets which would fly upwards when trodden on and, as the name implied, ensure that a hapless attacker might become, as the troops put it, a 'falsetto for the rest of his days'. This primitive minefield was backed up by running a wire inside at the rear. Along the wire, at regular intervals, were empty food cans filled with loose gravel from the track. If anyone managed to slip through the minefield unscathed, the tin cans would alarm the defenders to their presence.

He slumped back in his carriage-cum-headquarters, breathed out hard, feeling pretty drained of energy by his efforts and hoped he hadn't overlooked anything. In an hour he'd get his signaller to check in with Cadet Haas at the station round the bend. In some ways he now regretted sending the inexperienced cadet to carry out the task, but he reasoned, with two old hares such as Matz and Schulze under command, Haas would be able to cope.

'Yes,' he told himself, closing his eyes, 'I've done what I can . . . Matz and Schulze'll look after Haas. Before he knew it, von Dodenburg started to drift off into a gentle doze.

The woman was not surprised when Schulze came blundering in through the door of her *isba*, entering without knocking, a bundle of worthless occupation roubles in his big paw. He smiled at her as she continued to lie on a kind of divan, stretching out her long legs, clad in tight black trousers of the same silk-like material that all the local women seemed to wear.

She straightened her legs lazily and looked knowingly at the suddenly awed NCOs, who had not expected her to be so responsive. '*Raki*,' she said, pointing to the bottle of colourless spirit on the table next to the divan. She made a drinking gesture. The two didn't need urging.

'Rank hath its privileges,' Schulze growled, uncorked the bottle, took a hefty swing, coughed and replaced the stopper before throwing the bottle at Matz, who caught it neatly. He also drank and then they both stared at the woman, wondering how they would start this liaison; though she gave no indication that they would have problems with her when they did. Indeed, she seemed as if she would really welcome the attentions of two unshaven foreigners, smelling of sweat but definitely keen on the business of humping her nubile body if they got half a chance.

They didn't have to wait long to begin. She patted the divan in welcome and smiled, showing her single gold tooth proudly. She pointed at Matz.' '*Du?*' she asked in German.

Matz smiled but Schulze scowled. 'Hey,' he protested. 'None of that. I outrank him.'

It was doubtful that the woman understood his words, but she certainly understood what he wanted. '*Zusammen?**' she queried, patting both sides of the divan to make her meaning quite clear.

Her offer stopped both of them in their tracks. Matz looked at Schulze and the latter returned his look of bewilderment with, 'How are we gonna do that?'

On the divan, the woman slipped out of her silk trousers in anticipation, revealing a shapely, ivory-white body, surmounted by a tuff of jet-black hair. Slowly, very slowly, she parted her legs.

Schulze swallowed hard. 'Holy mackerel,' he said weakly, 'All that meat an' no potatoes! What we gonna do, Matzi?'

Matz forced his gaze away from the woman's body which glowed in the flickering light of the solitary candle. 'I don't know . . . But we'd better do it soon, Schulze, or I can't answer for the consequences. My fly buttons are beginning to pop already.'

The woman frowned. She opened her legs wider as if to urge them into immediate action.

Schulze said thickly, fascinated by the sight, 'We can toss for her.'

'You mean who goes first?'

'Yes.'

'All right. Have yer got a ten pfennig piece?'

Excited beyond all measure, all fingers and thumbs, Schulze fumbled for his lucky brass coin. On the divan, the woman licked her finger provocatively leaving no doubt about what she intended.

'Got it,' Schulze cried and put the coin on his thumb and forefinger, 'Call, you little apeturd!'

Matz said the first prayer he had uttered since he had left his Munich *schule* in disgrace for attempting to look up his teacher's skirt as a thirteen-year-old. '*Adler*†,' he said quickly.

'Heads,' Schulze said and breathed a fervent prayer too.

The woman raised her hips urging them, '*davoi*', as if she couldn't wait much longer. But neither she nor the two

*'Together'. *Transl.*

†ie. 'eagle' because the German ten pfennig coin bore an eagle on one side.

64

running mates were destined to enjoy the pleasures of the two-backed beast that night; for at the very instant that Schulze tossed the coin in the air, the night stillness shattered abruptly with the angry chatter of a machine gun. The two Wotan NCOs knew they were in trouble . . .

Three

Ox-Jo belched in pleasure and wiped the mutton fat from his thick red lips. He threw the bone over his shoulder at the half-starved hounds prowling around the damp fire. 'Not a bad bit of fodder.'

As an afterthought he took a handful of dry rice from the big cooking pot, looked around at the rest of the mountain troopers as if daring them to challenge him for eating their rations, and then stuffed the rice into his mouth.

'Better lay off the garlic, sarge,' one of the troopers said. 'Or we won't dare to light a match near your fart-cannon tonight.'

Ox-Jo smirked. 'Watch I don't light one in your arse, Breitmayr.' He picked his teeth and stared at the native woman who had served them. 'If it wasn't for that bastard, Greul, I'd have something better to kip with this night, but you might have to do instead.'

Breitmayr shut up quickly. You never knew when Ox-Jo was serious or joking. The big NCO was game for anything.

They had been marching most of the day; after they had slipped out of the ancient local trucks, which normally carried tea and the like over the Caucasian border into the tribal lands beyond, they found themselves in this tumbledown village, which seemed populated only by women and dirty, fat-bellied, barefoot children. According to Major Greul, who seemed to understand some of their native language, all the menfolk had been forcibly conscripted into the Red Army by raiding parties from the communist-held coast, leaving behind their women to tend to the animals and breed children. Not that the women looked like breeding types. They were slim and, beneath their shapeless gowns, they seemed athletic. Greul had warned them as he dismissed them to prepare their evening meal, 'I don't want you rogues attempting anything with these women. Not only would it be dangerous if their menfolk found out, you might catch—er . . .' Here the prudish major had flushed an embarrassed red, 'a social disease.'

Even Colonel Sturmer had been forced to chuckle at Greul's discomfort.

While the men ate and griped at their inability to enjoy the local women, Sturmer lay in his field bed. As weary as he was from that long march after leaving the tea lorries, he couldn't sleep. Opposite him, in the hut they shared, Greul was already snoring. Sturmer smiled. The prudish major could fall asleep at the drop of a hat; nothing worried him. Perhaps he didn't have a conscience – he certainly didn't have an imagination. 'Lucky swine,' Sturmer whispered to himself and pulled his sleeping bag up around his shoulders. The sun had vanished, it was growing cold quickly, which was understandable. They were getting ever closer to the snow-capped mountain that was their objective.

Outside, the village was settling down. Even the usual steady tread of the sentries was absent. Sturmer had taken a risk and posted none, for most of the men were bone weary after the long march. Besides there were only women in the place and they had offered the troopers food of their own accord. He had judged they were relatively safe here. Once the locals offered newcomers bread and salt, the traditional gift of friendship, one was usually safe from treachery.

Sturmer's mind turned to the plan. So far everything had gone well. In fact they had smuggled themselves out of the German zone of occupation on the coast into the interior without being – he hoped – noticed. Of course, they had previously encountered a few villages like this one but the natives were used to raiding and reconnaissance parties from both the Red Army and the *Wehrmacht*; troops penetrating the area temporarily in the search of recruits, forced labour or whatever else they might be interested in. Their passing had, Sturmer reasoned, occasioned no particular interest for the locals. The trick was to not stop in one place long enough for the natives to become curious.

Satisfied that everything had gone according to plan, Sturmer was beginning to concern himself with the rendezvous with von Dodenburg's light armour of SS Assault Battalion Wotan. Naturally, armour would cause interest; both sides so far had relied on foot soldiers and irregular cavalry in the Caucasus. Armour was a different thing altogether.

He frowned and listened momentarily to Greul's hearty snoring as he considered what was the best way to proceed once the rendezvous between the two elite units had taken place. The armour was essential to protect his right flank till he reached the starting point for the climb up to the summit of Mount Elbrus. It was a safety measure that he had to have for at least two days. Once his men had reached Elbrus House and he had picked his climbing teams, then he could look after any opposition. There was no unit in the Red Army – which, as far as he knew, didn't have alpine troops – that could match his brawny Bavarian mountaineers. He'd only need von Dodenburg's Wotan again at withdrawal, after planting the Nazi flag on the taller of the two peaks, or 'twin tits' as that cheeky Schulze had called them. By then he anticipated that the Reds would have tumbled what was going on and would try to stop them.

Sturmer lay motionless in his sleeping bag for a while; he wondered about the millions of soldiers, like himself, all over the world, also huddled in sleeping bags, lying in the open or sweating in the jungle, unable to sleep, tired as they might be, pondering the events of the morrow, knowing that the new dawn might bring misery and sudden violent death.

Somehow it all seemed suddenly purposeless. For what did all the suffering, the misery, the killing, prove in the end? Nothing. When the politicians failed to find their answers, ordinary men had to take over. They had to risk their lives in remote places in strange countries in order to solve the politicians' problems for them. And how did they do that? They did it, not with the honeyed, cynical talk of the politicians, but with the most brutal means possible – by killing.

Sturmer sighed. He dismissed the subject, one which sensitive soldiers have pondered without an answer for centuries, and tried to sleep. All he could hear was Greul's relentless snoring. Then it started to fade into the far distance. He was falling asleep at last; the last sound which impinged upon his awareness before he finally sank into the blessed oblivion of sleep was the soft chink-chink of what might have been a horse's hooves striking a rock. Then he was gone, snoring heartily himself . . .

Ox-Jo rubbed the front of his long johns. He farted and even though he was only half awake, he felt the pleasant sensation of an erection slowly beginning to develop. He farted again. In his sleep, the nearest trooper turned hurriedly to the opposite side. Even in his sleep, his nostrils were assailed and sickened by the foul smell. Ox-Jo chuckled. His erection grew. God, how he could go a woman now. He hadn't gotten the dirty water off his chest since they'd been in Warsaw nearly a week before. He told himself that if he went on like this, he'd be impotent before they got out of the Caucasus. Better go outside and have a piss. It was a shame to waste a diamond-cutter like he had now, but a piss would get rid of it and he could sleep in peace again. Reluctantly he got out of the warm sleeping bag, pulled on his mountain boots and then, as an afterthought, strapped on his pistol belt, and placed his cap on his head, and went outside.

All was silent. He took out his organ and started to urinate, the liquid steaming in a golden curve in the cold air. Slowly his erection began to disappear. But not quite. Even as he finished, it was still there; limp, but definitely there. Ox-Jo cursed and told himself that it wasn't fair on a man to have a diamond-cutter like that and not get rid of it because some holier-than-thou shit of an officer said it wasn't right to touch one of the native women. What did Greul know about a real man's needs.

Suddenly Ox-Jo made up his mind. He pulled his pistol belt tighter and bent down to tie the laces of his mountain boots. With a bit of luck he might strike lucky. At any event he might see a few pairs of tits, if he peered into the huts where the women were.

69

He started to ascend the rise where he had last seen the young women enter their huts. Under the cold velvety sky, a cold wind swept in from the mountains. It didn't worry Ox-Jo. His mind was full of lascivious thoughts which kept his half-clad body more than warm. He licked his lips. Heaven, arse and cloudburst, what wouldn't he give for a little bit of the other? Now he entered the deep shadows cast by the rock wall. Carefully, moving on the outside soles of his feet as he had been trained to do when attacking an enemy position, he approached the first *isba*, from which came the sound of light snoring. His evil face lit up. They'd be in there, perhaps stripped naked under the furs they used to cover themselves at night, lovely little bodies just made for mattress polka.

Cautiously, very cautiously, heart beating rapidly at the exciting thought of what he might see, the big Bavarian pushed aside the sacking which served as a door to the tumbledown *isba*. For a few moments he let his eyes become accustomed to the gloom of the interior, lit by a weak flickering tallow light.

He could smell the delightful sweet odour of young female bodies, which were not well washed. Not that such things worried Ox-Jo. His mind was strictly on other things. Then he made out the two girls sleeping in the far corner of the primitive cottage, next to the warmth of the big tiled oven which reached nearly to the ceiling.

Ox-Jo swallowed hard. Both of the girls, were clasped in each other's arms, the darker of the two with her hand on the other girl's breast. He felt the sudden tumescence in his loins and wished fervently he dare steal across to them and take them. But he knew he daren't. Greul would have him shot, the unfeeling prudish bastard.

But he feasted his eyes on the girls, praying that the one with her hand on the other's little breast with its pink-tipped nipple, might move their fur covering a little lower, to reveal more of those delightful nubile female bodies. But that wasn't to be and with the wind howling around his naked nether regions, Ox-Jo found even he was losing his sexual desire; it was too cold. It was time to get back to the warmth of his sleeping bag.

'Grr,' he breathed through gritted teeth, 'you don't know what you missed, girls. I could have given yer a treat—' One of the girls stirred and gave a little groan. She was waking up. It was time to go while he was still safe. Hastily, but reluctantly, Ox-Jo let the curtain drop and retreated backwards down the little path that led to the *isba*, keeping to the shadows like the good soldier that he was.

He didn't get far. The blow to the back of his head caught him completely by surprise. He staggered and went down, almost to his knees. Ox-Jo always boasted that he had a thick skull. He didn't go out as many a man would after such a tremendous blow. 'What the frig,' he yelped in pain.

This time his assailant didn't use the club. Instead a scarf, or something like it, was whipped around his neck as he struggled to regain his balance. It bit cruelly into his neck. Desperately his fingers sought that choking scarf. His ears drummed. A red mist rose. He was choking to death. But Ox-Jo was not fated to die just yet. As the red mist threatened to engulf him, a voice commanded in Russian, 'Let him live.' And that was the last Ox-Jo heard for a while, as that killing scarf was removed and he fell to the stony ground, unconscious before he reached it.

Swiftly his assailants, whoever they were, did what they had come here to do. First they whipped off the unconscious man's peaked cap with the silver *Edelweiss** badge. His special pistol came next and then, as an afterthought, one of his clumsy mountain boots was tugged off, with his assailants gagging at the stink that came from his unwashed feet.

Moments later they were gone with their strange booty, leaving an unconscious Ox-Jo lying prone and half-naked in the freezing night . . .

**Edelweiss*, a high mountain meadow flower, prized in the German alps and worn by men of the German mountain divisions.

Four

Old Leather Face, as the Soviet dictator was called behind his back, was smaller than most of the attending generals and corps commanders had expected. He was fatter too and although his dark Georgian eyes seemed to smile benevolently, as was to be expected of the Little Father as his subjects had to call him, those thick sensual lips revealed him as a man of passion, cruel passion, who at the click of his tobacco-stained fingers could send a whole set of people to the slavery and misery of the gulags and not give the matter a second thought.

He poked his dark pock-marked face with the stem of his pipe and said slowly, in the Georgian fashion, 'Comrade generals, I have called you here because of the situation in the Kuban and now in the Caucasus.'

The most important soldiers in the mighty Red Army, the most powerful army in the world, dropped their cropped heads like shamed schoolboys who had been caught out. Was Old Leather Face going to blame them for the failure of his own strategy? Was it the gulag for some of them?

Surprisingly enough the Soviet dictator didn't burst into one of his feared rages and begin blaming them for the disaster in the Kuban. Instead he said mildly, 'Comrade Generals, it is clear that as soon as the Fritzes start their offensive in the south in earnest, they will drive into the Caucasus in force. There are two reasons for that. I shall tell you them.'

Relieved, the high-ranking generals of the Southern Front looked at him with feigned interest as he took another puff at his curved pipe, which never seemed to disappear from his hands. Perhaps he thought it gave him a kindly avuncular look, which hid the cruel ogre that Stalin was in reality.

'One, as the basis of the Fritzes' long term strategy. Because we can expect them to attempt to link up with the Japs to the east and squeeze out India, which supplies the English with so many of its soldiers. Two, on a short-term basis, the Fritzes need oil for their armoured thrusts. Romania cannot supply them satisfactorily. So what's their answer?' He didn't give his generals time to attempt to respond.

'They'll be after our oil in the Caucasus.'

He let his words sink in before adding, 'To a certain extent we can afford to lose the Caucasian oil. However, a German victory there would set the region against us. Turkey, in particular, which has always been our enemy, would pose a grave threat to our southern flank, if the Turks decided, on the basis of a German victory, and the link they would have in Caucasus with the Fritzes, to throw in their lot with the Fritzes.' He paused momentarily and puffed at his pipe once more before saying, 'You understand, of course, comrade generals?'

There was a hasty murmur of agreement from the assembled officers. They knew that they always had to agree swiftly with Old Leather Face, for in the corner crouched his sinister hunchbacked secretary, Aleksandr Poskrebyshev, who was always on the lookout for subordinates who didn't seem to be alert to the dictator's every wish and whim.

Stalin waited until one of his servants entered to hand each general a small cloth soaked in eau-de-cologne which they dabbed on their faces to remove the sweat caused by the overheated room. Among themselves they knew this was not a Russian custom, but one from his own remote Georgian homeland. It signified – to those who dare even think of such matters – that Old Leather Face was not really one of them, a real Russian, but a member of a race that Mother Russia had once despised and conquered. But the tables had been turned, now Stalin and his Georgian cronies ruled Mother Russia.

Stalin let them dry their faces before continuing with the reason for summoning them so hastily to his headquarters. 'In the last few days, comrade generals, I have received disquieting news from the Caucasus. It seems that there are two Fritz columns entering the area. Both appear to be in battalion strength only so we cannot regard this as a major tactical move. However,' he took his pipe out of his mouth and pointed the stem at them, as if it were a deadly weapon, 'we must take this incursion seriously. It might well be a reconnaissance, in force for what is to come. The Fritzes are no fools. They plan their operations well, unlike some of my commanders.'

Colonel-General Kozlov, the most senior field officer there, flushed to the roots of his cropped hair. He pulled his tight-fitting tunic, heavy with the gold epaulettes of a general, as if he were about to go on parade, and said, 'With your permission, Comrade Secretary, we of the Southern Front are well prepared for anything the Fritzes and their *clever* tactics –' he emphasized the word deliberately – 'can throw at us.'

'Yes?'

'*Yes*, Comrade Secretary,' the broad-chested general went on, ignoring the cynical look on Stalin's face and the fact that the hunchbacked secretary was making a note in his ever-present notebook: a warning if there ever was one. 'I have the mass of two infantry armies, plus several independent army and artillery corps, plus armour packed around the bottle neck the Fritzes must use if they are going to attack in strength from the coast of the Black Sea.'

'I see, Comrade Colonel-General,' Stalin said coldly, 'that you are prepared to put all your eggs in one basket. Back in the summer of forty-one that was the downfall of too many of my generals, *your* comrades.'

Still Kozlov didn't heed the warning. 'I do not understand,' he started to question.

Stalin cut him short, sharply. 'Of course you don't. Do you think the Fritzes are such fools that they will use the mass of their attacking forces to move along the Black Sea coast into the Caucasus and allow themselves to be shot to pieces by your waiting armies? A kind of written invitation on a silver platter, eh? Of course they won't and if you think they will, you're a bigger fool than I thought you were.'

He didn't give the general time to react, though he was spluttering in such a red-faced rage that it looked as if he might explode and disintegrate at any moment. He continued, 'The Fritzes don't play that kind of damnfool game unlike my generals.' Old Leather Face clicked his brown-stained fingers. The hunchback reacted immediately. Even without any words being exchanged between him and his master, he seemed to know instinctively what Stalin wanted. He signalled to the flunkies clothed in their dark, pre-war uniform.

Two giant men lifted the heavy marble table, upon which the Czars had once signed prisoners' death warrants, and carried it across to where Stalin sat in his throne-like chair. The hunchback hobbled after them with the top secret map of the Kuban Caucasus area.

Dutifully he spread the map out in front of his master and weighted it at each end while Stalin waited; his generals wondered what he had up his sleeve now. The dictator knew more tricks than a hound had fleas, but then all those Georgians were like that, they told themselves: treacherous folk upon whom it wasn't wise to turn one's back if you didn't want to find a knife slid into it.

Without further ado, Stalin rapped his pipe on the Causcaus Mountains. 'Here,' he said, 'they have a reconnaissance party up there, I was told last night. Why?'

This time Kozlov beat him to it. 'Of what importance are the Fritzes in the mountains, Comrade Secretary? Those Caucasus heights are virtually impassable . . .'

'Did you never hear of Hannibal crossing the Alps in that famous Frunzle Academy of yours?' Stalin meant the main Red Army military academy.

'Naturally, Comrade Secretary. But Hannibal had merely to bother about elephants not tanks, comrade,' Kozlov answered tartly, knowing that he was risking not only his career but also his neck by standing up to Old Leather Face like this; the hunchback was scribbling away furiously. 'Nor did he have to provision and look after a whole army with shells, supplies and heavy artillery.'

The Colonel-General's argument seemed to cut no ice with

Stalin. 'All the same, he crossed the Alps in the dead of winter and kicked the shit out of the Romans, just as the Fritzes might do to you, Comrade General, if I weren't here to protect you from your own foolishness.'

Lieutenant-General Kerst, as methodical and precise as his German forefathers, who had come to Russia to serve the Czars, thought it was time to intervene before Kozlov got himself into even deeper trouble. He cleared his throat and said, 'May I ask, Comrade Secretary, what indication have you that the Germans are really attempting to cross the Caucasian Mountains?'

Stalin didn't answer directly this time. Instead he nodded to the hunchback secretary. Once more the little civilian reacted at once. He nodded to the nearest uniformed flunky.

He went out and returned almost immediately. In his arms he bore a cap, a boot and a pistol, complete with leather holster. Here and there the generals' mouths dropped open in wonder. One of them gasped *'Boshe moi . . .* what is this?'

But Stalin was enjoying tormenting his subordinates. Let them wait; he was not going to reveal what he already knew at once. By not doing so, he felt it gave him the aura of superiority, even omnipotence. It made his generals believe that he, the great Stalin, the Little Father of the Russian people, always knew just a little bit more than the rest.

It was only when his generals dared to shuffle their feet impatiently, that he spoke. 'Well, General Kerst, you are our German expert. What do you make of these items?'

Kerst, who didn't like to be reminded of his German origins, kept a tight hold of himself. Stalin was an tyrant, worse than any of the Czars, even the mad ones. He was unpredictable; anger him in the slightest and one could find oneself in a very tricky situation. Kerst picked up the peaked cap which up to a couple of nights before had belonged to Ox-Jo, sniffed at the scent of the Bavarian's boot and, as he did so, announced, 'This cap belongs to a member of a German mountain battalion, the *Gebirgsjäger*. You can tell that from the silver flower badge here.'

Stalin beamed. '*Horoscho*, Comrade General. Please carry on.'

'The boot is a special kind worn by these mountain troops, in particular by those who are employed in the high mountains.' Kerst took the pistol out of its holster but found nothing notable on it. He was about to return it to the holster when he spotted the name and number on the worn leather of the holster, '*Oberjager Mayr,*' he read aloud, and then added, '*Sturmgruppe Adler*'.

Stalin looked at the general, well aware that the latter was convinced he had discovered something of significance. 'Well?' he demanded. 'What do you make of it; eh?'

'I believe this equipment belongs, Comrade Secretary, to a special Fritz group; one which operates in the high mountain ranges—'

'In other words,' Stalin cut him short triumphantly, 'the Fritzes are using specialist troops for their mission across the mountains?'

'Yes, I am sure you are right, comrade.'

'Of course I am. So what is to stop more Fritz mountain troops following the route these special troops have blazed for them? I ask you that, comrade generals?'

They did not answer. It was too dangerous. Stalin had probably made up his mind what to do even before they had been summoned to the conference room. This was simply an exercise in humiliation for them to endure.

'So, what are we to do about it? We have plenty of ski-troops, all those Siberians we have brought from the East, but they aren't mountain troops. They would be of little use in the high mountains, if we attempt to stop those Fritzes up there. What therefore can we do?'

Again his generals remained silent, as Stalin knew they would; and again he demonstrated his all-embracing knowledge of which he was inordinately proud. 'We shall deploy my Red Eagles up there.'

'Red Eagles, Comrade Secretary?' Kozlov ventured. 'I have not heard of these men.'

Stalin chuckled and played his final ace. 'Of course you haven't, Comrade General. For they are *not* men,' he said.

Kozlov looked puzzled and wished he hadn't spoken.

But Stalin was too full of himself to notice. 'The Red Eagles are, in fact, *women* . . .'

Five

Dawn came slowly as if nature itself was reluctant to illuminate the harsh reality of the scene in front of von Dodenburg and his group. He wiped his smoke-grimed face and, as he tackled the rise, stared at what was left of the whistle-stop station. A thin wisp of smoke was rising stiffly into the air from the burned-out shade. The bodies of Haas's men were laid out stiffly all around, as if they had been placed there to order to be taken away in due course. Von Dodenburg knew what that meant. Haas's men had surrendered – fools that they had been – and had been massacred out of hand, mown down in cold blood.

Von Dodenburg put his hand on top of his helmet, fingers outspread. It was the infantry signal for his men to advance. To left and right flank, the two self-propelled guns started up with a throaty roar, their trucks clattering on the rocky slope, their gunners crouched behind their protective armour, on the alert for any suspicious movements.

The firing had commenced two hours before. Von Dodenburg had identified its source immediately. It wasn't difficult; it was Russian, partisan probably or Caucasian irregulars. There was no mistaking the slow rat-tat of an old-fashioned Soviet machine gun; it sounded like the work of an irate woodpecker and it had come from the station to which he had sent Haas and his troop earlier. He had been alarmed for a few minutes. Cadet Haas was such a greenhorn after all. But then he had reassured himself that Hass was supported by the best of his old hares, Matz and Schulze. They knew the ropes; they had come under attack time and time again.

For that reason he had hesitated to send a relief party.

After all, to venture into the pitch darkness over unknown terrain was tantamount to looking for trouble. That was the sort of thing that Russian partisans or irregulars would expect panicked Germans to do – and they might walk straight into an ambush already prepared for any relief party.

After half an hour passed he could tell by the increased volume of Russian fire and the weakening of any response, that Hass and his men were in trouble. It was then that he decided he'd have to run the risk of walking into a trap and relieve the young cadet and his small troop of men.

By the time he had reached the halfway mark and dispatched his self-propelled gun to left and right, firing as they went to indicate to anyone lying in wait that they were facing armour, von Dodenburg knew with a sinking feeling that he was already too late. Apart from the few quick bursts from Schmeissers – high-pitched hysterical bursts that were typical of the German machine pistol – the defensive firing from the whistle-stop station had almost ceased. He could have also sworn he heard the sound of horses moving at speed. Now, as he poised in the ugly white light of the false dawn, even the splatter of Schmeisser fire had died away.

Fifteen or so minutes later, they advanced cautiously, through a line of Wotan soldiers who had surrendered and had been murdered in cold blood; the backs of their heads blown off with a final pistol shot, the shattered bones of the men glittering in the red gore like polished ivory. Von Dodenburg was plagued by an awed, frightening feeling that there was worse to come; partisans were known for their savage cruelty to the German enemy and to their own people.

The young arrogant SS officer was not mistaken. They turned the corner in the still smouldering station, by what looked like a wood store, and came to a sudden stop.

'Oh Holy Mother of God!' one of von Dodenburg's men cried out loudly, while the others recoiled, eyes suddenly full of abject horror. A Wotan trooper, totally naked, had been nailed to the door, arms outstretched like some latterday Jesus, his young head surmounted with a crown, not of thorns, but of barbed wire, the prongs pressing into his brow and

80

drawing blood, which now dripped down his dead face on to his naked shoulders.

Von Dodenburg swallowed hard. Just in time he stopped himself from vomiting, repressing the evil bile which threatened to choke him. 'What kind of people could do—' He stopped short. It was no use raging against fate. Here in Russia men had turned into beasts on both sides of the front. The winter war had brutalized them. Men like these should not survive; they'd be a danger to those at home for they'd never overcome what they had experienced and done in Russia. They were not beasts. They were worse; they were devils.

Minutes later they found Haas's dead body. He, too, was naked. But being an officer, the Russians had treated him even worse. Though he could barely look at the terribly mutilated body himself, von Dodenburg still had the strength to order his NCOs, his voice thick with rage and horror, 'Get the men out of here. For God's sake don't let them see Cadet Haas like that. *Now.*'

The NCO, who was already gagging, held his hand to his mouth to prevent himself being sick on the spot. He stumbled backwards, leaving von Dodenburg to carry out a task that he, who had seen much of the horrors of war since 1939 and who had thought he was hardened to almost everything, including cleaning out the charred remains of tank crews from their burned-out vehicles, could hardly bear to do.

Gingerly he forced the dead boy's jaw open a little wider. Wishing fervently that he could simply turn and run, but commanding himself not to do so, he took a grip of the piece of Haas's body which the Russians had cut off and inserted between his dead lips and pulled it free. For a moment he stood there, shaking wildly, as if he were afflicted by some tropical fever, wondering what he should do with the cadet's penis. Finally, he walked a pace forward and dropped it behind him. Then, as the hot green bile welled up inside him and he knew he couldn't stop himself being violently sick, he took his handkerchief out and dropped it over Haas's bloody loins. The next moment he fled outside and, leaning against the charred wall for support, his shoulders heaving

81

like those of a child carried away by inconsolable grief, he retched and retched and retched . . .

Later, after the NCOs had carried out a body count and had thrown a few handfuls of dirt over the dead, von Dodenburg, his face still ashen and almost feverish, realized that Schulze and Matz – as he had half expected – were not among the dead. Somehow the two old hares had escaped the massacre at the whistle-stop station.

Pulling himself together the best he could, he gave out his orders. The self-propelled gun would advance on the still silent Caucasian village while the troops formed up in a 'grape' behind it. The 'grape' would offer them the protection, at least to their front, if there were still insurgents waiting for them.

Slowly, the men advanced, their hands gripping their weapons, wet with sweat despite the dawn cold, each man wrapped up in a cocoon of his own thoughts and apprehensions. Von Dodenburg, starting to burn with rage again, did not attempt to take advantage of the cover offered by the 'grape'. Instead he strode forward, machine pistol at the ready, parallel with the front of the SP. His gaze flickered from left and right, as if he were daring the men who had massacred poor Cadet Haas to make an appearance so that he could blast them to eternity with his weapon. But none appeared. As they got closer to the village, and could see the smoke beginning to appear from beyond the roofs as the women-folk started to cook, and hear the first barks of the villagers' alarmed dogs, von Dodenburg told himself that the insurgents, whoever they had been, had vanished. If they had still been there, waiting for him and his men, the villagers would have quietly disappeared into the nearby village fields or the low hills beyond. He started to relax.

But at the same time, his concern for Schulze and Matz grew, mixed with a sense of bewilderment. Perhaps they had survived. But where in three devils' name were the two rogues?

He was soon to find out. From the turret of the self-propelled gun, which provided a better view than von Dodenburg had on the ground, the gun commander suddenly yelled, '*Wer da*? . . .' and then in Russian, '*Stoi*?' The driver below reacted automatically. He braked and the gunner manning the machine gun next to him, swung it round to face whoever the tank commander had just spotted.

'What's the trouble . . .?' von Dodenburg began, but the words died on his lips when he spotted the two figures which had caused the tank commander to halt his big cumbersome vehicle.

Two peasant women were coming towards them, slow and hesitant, one of them trailing a too long skirt behind and, so it appeared to von Dodenburg, carrying a German Mauser rifle over their shoulder. He jerked up his own weapon instinctively, ready to kill them on the spot, women or not after what he had seen back at the station. '*Ruki verze!*' Hands up,' he yelled harshly.

The bigger of the two obeyed immediately. The smaller of the two hesitated. But only for a fraction of a second; the officer's intention was only too clear and threatening. The smaller figure threw up his hands as well, the long skirt falling off to reveal a pair of rolled-up trousers and a pair of pale skinny legs – clad in regulation *Wehrmacht* dice-beakers*.

Von Dodenburg's mouth dropped open like that of some half-witted yokel. The 'woman' with the Mauser rifle was Corporal Matz and it was clear, as his companion began to whip off his headdress and the customary half veil of the Caucasian women, that the dress concealed the mighty bulk of Frau Schulze's handsome son, Schulze.

Von Dodenburg was caught completely by surprise by the two apparitions, 'Holy strawsack!' he exclaimed, '*you two*.'

Schulze and Matz didn't look particularly happy at being discovered wearing women's dresses. Matz said hastily, 'We had to do it, sir. It was the only way. Otherwise . . .' His words trailed away to nothing. Von Dodenburg guessed that they had been negligent in their duties but was relieved they had survived. If they had been where they should have been with Haas, they would probably have been dead now. 'Don't

*SS slang for their jackboots. *Transl.*

83

tell me now . . . You can explain later. For the time being, you can consider yourselves under open arrest. *Los*, we have other things to do.'

The two rogues looked mightily relieved. Hastily they whipped off the rest of the female clothes, which the woman on the divan had given them after they had become aware of the insurgents entering the village. Darting from house to house their enemy had checked the *isbas* before setting up their trap at the whistle-stop station.

Von Dodenburg wasted neither time nor pity on the handful of villagers,

Hastily they were routed out of their huts. Wailing and crying, pleading for their children, they were forced out into the dawn cold. The angry Wotan troopers were totally ruthless. After what they had just seen, even the most soft-hearted of the young SS men had no sympathy for these women whose lives were now going to be destroyed. Mercilessly they kicked over their cooking pots, stamped on their fires, here and there showing their utter contempt for the natives by ripping open their flies and urinating in their water jugs, while others tossed stick grenades into the village's sole well to destroy the supply.

Satisfied that there was no one left lurking in the village, von Dodenburg ordered the sobbing women and wailing children to be herded to the dirt square at the village's centre. His rage was great, but he didn't want the blood of these civilians on his hands, even if they might have helped the partisans. But he planned to destroy their homes and pathetic few possessions as a lesson they wouldn't forget.

A somewhat shame-faced Sergeant Schulze took over – for he realized now he should have attempted with Matz to help the men, trapped and then slaughtered at the station, instead of hiding in the woman's cottage. He clicked on his cigarette-lighter and ignited a bundle of dry hay. Next to him stood a waiting Matz, ready to hand over the bundles to the other Wotan troopers.

Von Dodenburg reflected for a moment. He was remembering what his father, a general, had said to him when Germany had fought its way into Russia in the First World

War; rampaging and burning deep into that enormous country. His father had said, 'Perhaps it was the only way to do it, Kuno, my boy. I don't know. But it left an ugly taste in one's mouth and also the knowledge that the native Russians would remember that we Germans came that way for a hundred years to come and would never forget what we had done to them. One day they would pay us back for it.'

Von Dodenburg dismissed that unsettling thought. He had to avenge his dead, tortured young soldiers. 'Schulze – burn them!' he called loud and clearly.

Schulze, who wanted to get away from this place as soon as possible, didn't hesitate. He lit the hay and it blossomed into red life at once. Matz started handing out the burning brands to the waiting troopers.

Suddenly they were running from hut to hut, yelling like a bunch of crazy Red Indians in the wild west films they had enjoyed in their youth, thrusting the flaming torches through the doors, tossing them onto the straw roofs. Tinder dry and heavy with resin, the tumbledown *isbas* began to burn immediately. Behind them in the little square, guarded by a couple of troopers armed with Schmeissers, the women huddled closer together, weeping and wailing, some of them throwing dirt into their faces as if they were mourning their dead. The children followed suit. Even babies sucking at their mother's nipples seemed to be affected and stopped their feeding.

Thick black smoke started to ascend straight into the hard-blue, unfeeling morning sky. The woman who had hidden the two NCOs rose and tried to break through the guards. Perhaps she wanted to appeal to Schulze to stop the burning. She didn't get a chance. One of the boy guards slammed the metal butt of his Schmeisser into her face. She screamed once and reeled back, her face looking as if someone had suddenly thrown a handful of strawberry jam into it. Schulze looked away as she sank to the ground, holding her ruined nose, the blood streaming through her clenched fingers.

Finally it was over and the troopers carrying the torches paused in their destructive work, chests heaving with the effort of running back and forth, sapped of all energy, as if someone had opened an unseen tap and it had run out, like water.

Schulze looked at his feet; almost as if that giant NCO, who could never be shamed, *was* ashamed for the first time. Matz stepped a few paces forward as if he were about to help the woman who had protected them and then stopped, knowing it was better he didn't do so.

Von Dodenburg had seen enough. His rage had vanished and was replaced by a vague sense of disquiet; he tried not to listen as his troopers shot the village animals. He knew, in a way, that he was condemning these women and their children to death up here in the high mountains, where it was difficult enough to find food as it was. Their homes were destroyed, as were whatever stores of food they had accumulated. Now his men were finishing off their animals from which the villagers might have bred for the next season.

His voice low and somehow dispirited, he ordered, 'All right, men, break off the action . . . Move out now in battle formation.'

'Back to the train, sir?' Schulze asked in an equally low voice.

Von Dodenburg shook his head. 'No, we haven't time for that. We'll pack everyone into the SPs till we reach the next railhead.'

'But—' Schulze began.

Von Dodenburg cut him short, almost angrily, 'You heard what I said, Sergeant.'

'Sir.'

While the men loaded up and the rest of the SPs were summoned by radio, von Dodenburg thought again of what his father, the general, had said: how the Russians would remember the Germans had come this way for a hundred years.

'By God,' the words of one of his troopers cut into his reverie, 'By Christ and all His Apostles, the towelheads'll certain remember us Germans for this, comrades.'

Von Dodenburg bit his bottom lip. He told himself they would. They'd curse the Germans, not only in this genera-tion, but for generations to come. Not only in this remote

God-forsaken place, but perhaps all over Europe, even all over the world.

Then they were moving, leaving the village to burn behind them, heading into the unknown, shoulders bent as they crouched on the swaying vehicles, as if weighed down by an intolerable burden which they would only rid themselves when they were dead.

PART THREE
The Red Eagles

One

O n the second day of their road march, von Dodenburg's column was ordered by Army HQ in Maikop to turn sharply eastwards and leave the coastal foothills. Von Dodenburg was worried by the fuel supply – the self-propelled guns, weighing over 20 ton, ate up fuel greedily – but he was advised that that would be taken care of in due course. So the little column rolled east at a steady ten kilometres an hour, with von Dodenburg conserving his diesel carefully. Over the years of combat von Dodenburg had come to be cynical about the promises of high command.

Schulze and Matz were at the point, on a three-wheeled motorcycle of the type adapted to the rough conditions of the Soviet roads – or the lack of them. Surprisingly the two old hares, who always advised their fellow NCOs never to volunteer for anything except for the first turn in a knocking shop, had volunteered for the dangerous and bone-shaking task. It was something that puzzled von Dodenburg but then he didn't know that the two rogues still felt a sense of shame for their behaviour at the station, where the young troopers under Cadet Haas had been massacred.

Still, as they moved slowly eastwards towards the snow-capped peaks in the far distance, von Dodenburg relaxed a little. The countryside, which seemed deserted of human-kind, even of wild animals, was beautiful. Long grassy stretches reaching to the horizon with none of that under-lying menace of the steppe and, as von Dodenburg noted automatically, very few trees – save for the occasional grove of stunted olive trees – in which partisans and other irregulars could hide. As he sprawled on the warm deck of the leading self-propelled, listening to the idle soft chat of the other Wotan troopers lying there, he felt this journey could go on for ever. Time out of war was something the Führer's Firebrigade, SS Assault Regiment Wotan, rarely enjoyed.

But now and again there were reminders of what lay ahead of them. Catching up with a battered Schulze, astraddle his motorbike, von Dodenburg asked, 'Where's the fire, you big rogue?'

Schulze wiped the scum of his cracked parched lips and, thrusting his goggles to his forehead to reveal two saucer-like eyes, surrounded by grey dust, the big NCO answered, 'Look at that in the far distance. At three o'clock.'

Von Dodenburg turned in the direction indicated and put his binoculars to his eyes. A tall, glistening white peak slid into the centre of the calibrated glass. Hurriedly he focused the binoculars. There was something awesome, even majestic, about the sight and for some reason he couldn't speak for a moment until Schulze, busy unscrewing the cap of his water-bottle asked, 'Do you think that's it, sir?'

Von Dodenburg knew what he meant. 'Yes, that's it all right, Schulze. That's the mountain . . . that's Elbrus.'

Schulze took a slug and whistled softly. 'Big bastard,' he commented.

'Big bastard it is,' von Dodenburg replied. As Schulze kick-started the awkward-looking bike and Matz clung on to his waist, he told himself that Sturmer, wherever he was, was going to have his work cut out to conquer that mountain, even under peace time conditions.

It was that same day that von Dodenburg was reminded yet again that this was not a peace time tour of a remote exotic land, but a wartime expedition. The men had just settled down before last light to cook their frugal supper of 'fart soup', when the sentry raised the alarm. Urgently the young Wotan trooper shouted, 'Plane at one o'clock . . . plane at one o'clock!'

Immediately they swung their gaze to the right, shading their eyes against the sunrays. Even before he spotted the little plane in the far distance, von Dodenburg knew what it was. The men called it 'the sewing machine', for its engine made a tick-tack sound like a treadle sewing machine. Its real name, however, was the 'Rata', and it was used by the Red Air Force as a low-level slow-moving spotter and ground reconnaissance machine.

They waited anxiously, wondering if the little plane would turn in their direction and sight them. The Rata seemed to hover in the sky, like some mechanical hawk, trying to pinpoint its victim. Then it broke to port abruptly, swooping low and dragging its shadow across the plain.

Von Dodenburg tensed. The gunners on the SPs pulled back the triggers of their machine guns and cocked them. Von Dodenburg nodded his head in approval. If the Rata came their way, the only thing left for them to do was to knock the damned plane out of the sky and move hell-for-leather, before the Popovs became aware of the fact and sent another one to check what had happened. It wasn't the best of solutions, but the only one he could think of at the moment.

They waited nervously, hardly daring to breathe, as the little plane headed slowly in their direction. Hardly recognizing his own voice, von Dodenburg heard himself order, 'Prepare to fire.'

The seconds seemed to creep leadenly. Von Dodenburg could feel the cold sweat of apprehension trickle down the small of his back unpleasantly. Then suddenly, startlingly, it happened. The throaty noise of a powerful engine being started was heard. The abrupt stink of gasoline. He flung a look to his front It was Schulze; he had driven the strange-looking motorbike out of the gully in which he had hidden it and was racing wildly across the plain, throwing up a huge cloud of dust behind him. On the pillion seat, Matz was madly trying to unsling his machine pistol and avoid being thrown off the bike at the same time.

'In God's name, Schulze,' The words von Dodenburg uttered died on his lips. Suddenly he realized what the big rogue was up to. He was attempting to draw the Rata away from their convoy. Indeed Schulze and Matz were risking their very lives to save the rest. What von Dodenburg didn't realize at that tense moment was that the two NCOs were attempting to carry out a kind of act of atonement for their neglect of duty at the station.

Suddenly the pilot of the little Russian plane spotted the motorcycle bolting and bucking across the plain. He increased his speed. Matz loosed off a burst of fire. The watchers could see the white tracer zipping across the blue sky; naturally Matz hadn't much chance of hitting the plane under those conditions but he certainly rattled the pilot. He veered wildly to the left, as the troop watched in anticipation.

Again von Dodenburg tensed. What would the pilot do next? It was clear that he was being deflected by Matz's wild fire from the course which would have led him directly over the stalled convoy. But would he flee? Or would he carry out his reconnaissance mission?

He did neither. Obviously Matz's fire had both rattled and annoyed him. He came around in a tight turn. Abruptly he dived. The single machine gun mounted on the Rata's wing spat fire. The watchers held their breaths as they saw the white and green tracer zipping towards the flying motorbike. Schulze, the old hare, knew what to do. He increased his speed. In a wild whirling wake of flying dust, he zig-zagged from side to side . . .

The watching troopers broke their awed silence. They cheered the two bold NCOs on. 'Show the bastard,' they cried. 'Come on Sergeant Schulze, blow him one of yer wet farts . . . Knock the Popov prick outa the sky . . . *dalli . . . dalli!*'

Unwittingly the men on the motorbike were going to do exactly that. As if carried away by a blind rage that made him forget the rules of flying, the Russian pilot came down to almost ground level. His prop wash lashed the grass of the steppe from side to side just in the same instant that Schulze changed direction abruptly. He wrenched the handlebars round and headed straight for one of the groves of stunted, twisted olive trees.

The Russian pilot saw his mistake too late. As Schulze entered the wood, avoiding slamming into the trees by some miracle, the Russian tried to pull up the plane. The watchers could see him straining at the joystick with all his might. He seemed to be standing upright in the cockpit, tugging desperately at it – to no avail. Suddenly he let go. As if in despair he threw his hands in front of his face.

In vain. The little Rata slammed into one of the olives. For a second or so it careened forward, the sound of rending, tearing metal clearly audible to the cheering men on the ground. The Rata's wings came off; left and right. It was as if some giant had torn the wings off some metallic beetle. The wrecked plane exploded in a blinding flash of light. Schulze and Matz came wheeling slowly out of the grove of olives, standing upright in their saddles shaking their clasped fists above their heads as if they were Max Schmeling after his defeat of the American 'Brown Bomber', Joe Louis, back before the war.

Perhaps an hour later or thereabouts, as von Dodenburg worried the Russians might have sent up another plane to look for the missing Rata, the sky to the south-east became slowly noisy with the sound of several planes approaching at low level. Von Dodenburg's heart jumped. The Russians had spotted them after all! They were sending in their dive-bombers, the dread Stormoviks; and out here on the almost featureless plain, without cover, they'd hardly have a chance. 'Stand by, gunners,' he ordered, tapping the mike strapped to his chest, 'prepare for air– –'

The order died on his lips. To the south-east, from which the sound of the plane engines came, red, green, and again red signal flares hissed into the cloudless afternoon sky. Von Dodenburg's face lit up. The pattern of red, green and red again was Wotan's own signal. The oncoming planes were friends. He realized, as the first 'Auntie Jus' – the trusty old Junkers 52s, the supply workhorse of the *Luftwaffe* – appeared overhead and the first parachutes started to blossom forth, pushed out by their handlers, that this was the promised supply mission of diesel, food and ammunition. For once the Luftwaffe was living up to its promise to the poor old stubble-hoppers below.

'All right,' von Dodenburg commanded eagerly, as the surprised convoy rolled to a stop. 'Get moving, boys. We don't want to hang around here too long.'

His men needed no urging. They knew that these supply drops often contained pleasant surprises supposedly from Fat Hermann* himself. At least there was a photograph of the air marshal, in all his bemedalled splendour, with them and the legend attached in his own handwriting, 'For my boys. Best of luck, men!' They dropped over the sides of their vehicles and ran forward like eager schoolboys released from school after a long boring day in the classroom. Eagerly, faces radiant, arms upstretched as if taking part in some schoolboy's game, they caught the parachutes and deftly unbuckled the shrouds fastening them to the wicker baskets and long metal tubes; the food bombs as they were called. Under the direction of the NCOs, in particular Schulze and Matz, their sins now atoned, they ripped open the containers, while von Dodenburg unwrapped the message dropped by the single-winged Fiesler Storch, which guided the 'Auntie Jus' to their DZ.

Hastily von Dodenburg's eyes skimmed the message. The first sentences informed him of the map reference where he was to join with Sturmer's mountaineers, some twenty or thirty kilometres to the north-west. That was routine. The next paragraph was not so welcome. It read, '*Luftwaffe* intelligence has intercepted signals detailing search for SS Regiment Wotan. A matter of urgency to contact Sturmer as soon as possible.' There was a scribbled signature below, which von Dodenburg couldn't decipher. Below, however, the pilot who had dropped the message had written in pencil, 'Just keep your chins up. There are worse things at sea.' A suddenly despondent von Dodenburg doubted it at that moment. As he watched the antiquated lumbering transport planes turn slowly and head back to their base, he felt a sensation of loneliness, even abandonment. It was as if the last link with the army, even the Homeland, was being severed and he feared that, for some reason he couldn't make out, he would never see either again.

Schulze and Matz gazed in disgust at the foodbomb which they had hoped would contain some of Fat Hermann's

---

* The exceedingly fat head of the Luftwaffe, Hermann Goering.

goodies; perhaps a link of good German salami, or perhaps even a bottle of Korn. Instead they now gazed in forlorn bewilderment at the box adorned with the air marshal's pudgy-faced photo and bearing the legend, 'Volcano, Special Rubber Products for the Protection of Soldiers of the Greater German Armed Force.'

Matz spat drily. 'Frigging Parisians,' he commented at last. 'French letters.' What does that frigging Fat Hermann think we're going to do out here in Popovland, fuck the Ivans to death?'

To that overwhelming question, not even Sergeant Schulze had an answer.

Two

Major Mikailovna, of the elite female Red Eagles, had been exactly ten years old in 1917 when the Revolution had broken out; it had changed her world. Although her father had been middle-class and a mixture of liberal and conservative, the Whites had murdered him after he had protested against their excesses. Her mother, half crazed by his death and addicted to vodka and morphine, had gone with a gang of soldier-bandits who had lived off terrorizing and looting the Kulaks. Then she had disappeared from her daughter's world for good. One of the thousands, hundreds of thousands, who had perished in the cruel years of the civil war that followed the 1917 Revolution.

Somehow the teenage girl had survived. Months on end she starved or lived off beets and frozen potatoes stolen from the fields, fighting off the men of all races and classes who tried to seduce the pretty blonde virgin. In the end the Reds, whom she had helped as a kind of child spy, carrying intelligence back and forth through enemy lines, had taken pity on the skinny girl. They had managed to get her into a state orphanage as a 'ward of the war', where for the first time she ate enough and could wash herself, returning to lessons which she had almost forgotten.

She had spent the next decade in such institutions until she had been sent to one of the new Sports' Universities modelled on similar ones in Germany. Here she had developed her magnificent body which was the envy of her fellow students, both male and female, and she had worked all out to obtain the coveted 'Master of Soviet Sport'.

Without complaint, hardened by those three years as a starving child in the wartorn villages with, it seemed, every man's hand against her, she had survived the killing routine of the degree course. The six o'clock bugle, the old-fashioned Swedish drill before a breakfast of black bread, milk and sugarless tea; the long sweating hours in the gym, the endless afternoons of all the modern sports, fistball, basketball and numerous other new forms of exercise introduced from the decadent West. She had never weakened. While her comrades, male and female, had been glass-eyed and weak-kneed with exhaustion by the end of the day, tottering off to their spartan barracks to collapse onto their bunks, she still had reserves of energy left, devoting herself to reading the latest technical sports manuals.

In 1930, with the Soviet Union seemingly prospering and, at least for young people, a new hope in the air, she had accepted the invitation of her male student friends to join an expedition to the remote Caucasian mountains. They were going to climb there; a sport reserved for men. She, for her part, would be in charge of the base camp. There she would ensure they were fed properly, had all their climbing equipment ready in the morning and, as one handsome blond young man assured her, 'Make us happy in the evening, if you know what I mean.' He had winked significantly and she had given him such a friendly push that he had been nearly knocked off his feet.

She had enjoyed the routine and especially the beauty of the mountains at first, but after a week had passed, with her restless nature, she had longed to do something more active. Although she knew mountaineering was regarded as the perogative of the male of the species, she asked her companions if she could go on a climb to 'carry the cooking pots, please' as she had put it demurely.

She did more than carry the cooking pots. Somehow or other, she couldn't remember exactly afterwards – it was something to do with one of the students being afflicted by mountain sickness, an ailment she had never heard of before – she found herself that day dangling at the end of a rope on a sheer mountain face. There she proved to be a pillar of strength, equal in stamina to the fit young men who were with her. Afterwards, lolling in the grass, damp with sweat, the young men enjoyed the relief of having conquered the peak, glad to have survived, even with a weak woman as part of their team. The young men looked at her almost with awe. As the team leader breathed heavily, dabbing the sweat from his handsome young face, he exclaimed. 'Comrade, I think after this, the mountains will have to look out!'

She had dabbed her bloody knees, not seeming to notice the glances of the men at her shapely legs, and had breathed modestly, 'Thank you very much, comrade.'

'Don't thank me, comrade.' The team leader had laughed. 'We thank you.' The boy, who would die young by a German bullet through his head on the first day of the German invasion of June 1941, had added thoughtfully, 'But remember this, comrade, mountains are not there to be conquered . . . they are there to be loved, too.'

She had always remembered those words. She *would* always love the mountains even though in the years to come she would spend all her free time and her meagre sports teacher's pay at academy conquering new peaks, moving from the smaller ones to those which even experienced mountaineers hesitated to tackle. The Soviet press started to take notice of her. The party organ, *Pravda*, called her 'the new Soviet woman'. *Trud*, the trade union paper, maintained that 'every Soviet worker and peasant must follow her career with admiration and emulation'. The *Ivestia* even sent journalists and photographers to cover one of her easier climbs. Her motto was uttered for the Soviet weekly newsreel shown everywhere in that great land; '*Nada Vetserapat*' – never give up – was adopted by the youth groups of the *Komosl* everywhere.

By 1935 she had become one of the Soviet Union's best known women. A year later she had been personally received by no less a person than Comrade Stalin, the Soviet dictator. He had pinned the order of the Red Star to her firm chest, kissed her on both cheeks and had pressed his hands to her tight muscular buttocks as he had done so, before remarking afterwards to his sinister chief-of-secret-police, Beria, 'Lavrenti Pavlovich, I could think of a better occupation for that particular young woman than climbing mountains,'

The secret policeman, known for his taste for young teenage virgins, had adjusted his pince-nez, and sniggered, 'I know . . . I know . . . On her back naked with her legs spread as wide as they would go.'

It had been the dictator's turn to snigger. '*Da . . . da . . .* only I fear comrade, with those tremendous thigh muscles of hers, she'd crush this poor old man to death.' And the two old lechers had burst into laughter while the proud young mountaineer had waved enthusiastically to the marching crowd passing through Moscow's Red Square below.

That year she had begun to enjoy herself for the first time. She had made a name for herself; she was known throughout the Soviet Union and she had also been received and honoured by the Little Father, Stalin, himself. Some thought her, with her trim muscular figure and black cropped hair, to be a lesbian as many Soviet female athletes were. Others thought, with her background, she had to be a blue stocking, one of the Russian feminists who detested men and lived for the cause of the 'new Soviet woman'.

In fact she was neither. She liked men and she liked fashionable clothes. She even bought the smuggled-in European fashion magazines on the Moscow black market and employed seamstresses to make her copies of the latest fashions from Paris, London and Berlin.

Naturally there were men who wanted to marry her. But in many cases they were middle-aged party officials who only realized the importance of her fame to them and the fact that she was pretty – and there was no denying that the senior party bosses liked pretty, well-dressed women instead of their usual *babuskha**-like wives, especially if some obliging lower-class officials would 'lend her out' for a night of sex.

She wanted none of that kind of so-called 'Party Marriage'. She thought of herself – naturally – as a patriotic loyal Russian woman who owed everything to the Soviet State. After all it had taken her, as a half-starved orphan girl, trained and educated her, and allowed her to do the thing she loved most:

*Grandmother. *Transl.*

101

climb mountains. She felt she had to set an example to all those other downtrodden Russian women, who were often beaten by their new husbands; men who had gone to bed, on their honeymoon, blind drunk and had raped their new wives as if they were the cheap whores that they had frequented previously.

So, although there were a few fleeting romances in the years before the war, she had concentrated on the mountains, facing ever-more challenging and dangerous sheer faces, feeling almost a sexual excitement, a strange tingling between her shapely muscular legs when she had conquered another difficult, exhausting climb. Indeed she half-realized that by climbing she was able to sublimate her sexual desires.

The war had caught her completely by surprise. When it came, she realized abruptly how selfish she had been, devoting herself to the mountains and her own advancement without a care for what was happening in the outside world. She had volunteered the very same day that the Fritzes had crossed the Russian frontier and had started their march on Moscow.

She had driven to the nearest Soviet Army post, hidden her little car behind the building and snapped to attention to the local political commissar. She had said gruffly, in an uneducated accent, 'Comrade, I wish to join the Red Army. *Now!*'

The commissar, a middle-aged, greasy-looking individual, had licked his lips as he eyed her and her splendid figure. 'Yes. *Horoscho*, you can become my cook and assistant when we go to the front.' He had smirked. 'It will be easy. I shall place you under my personal protection, if you follow me, comrade?'

She had, only too well. He wanted her to become his field mattress, as the soldiers called those women who became the mistresses of high officials and officers while they were at the front. 'No,' she had snapped. 'I want to *fight!*'

And fight she had. At first it had been difficult but as the Red Army's casualties had mounted, the generals in charge had had no compunctions about employing women in the firing line. She had become a sniper. The first time she had killed a Fritz, lining up his stupid German skull in her telescopic sight and watching as the bullet had smashed into it, the man's head disintegrating in a red flurry of blood and gore, she had been sick. But that had been the first time. Thereafter it had become easy; often too easy, she had told herself.

By mid-September she had been promoted to lieutenant in charge of a whole section of female snipers and then when the *Stavka*, the Russian High Command, wanted to use her for propaganda purposes, the powers-that-be had discovered who she really was. It was then that Stalin himself had ordered her to form a female battalion of climbers, novices as well as experts, to be used in the high mountains. Thus the Red Eagles, the only female alpine battalion in the whole of the Red Army, had been born. Still there had been sceptics. 'What good were women in combat?' the traditionalists had queried, 'save as nurses or snipers?' Time and time again Mikailovna had pleaded with them to 'give my girls a chance'. In the end the *Stavka* had given way. On the last night of December 1941, she and her most experienced climbers had climbed the 'Pimple' at the besieged city of Leningrad and had assassinated the German divisional commander and his staff in their own beds. They had escaped back to their own lines without a single casualty.*

A week later they had been sent to the Urals, the Russians' last defence at that time, on another assassination mission. It had failed this time, for which she had been glad – she didn't like these 'murder missions', as she called them to herself. But the failed attempt of the life of a senior German corps commander had given the enemy pause. They had begun to see assassination squads behind every tree. Stalin had personally ordered the Red Eagles to Moscow. There they had paraded in front of the massed newsreel cameras while the Little Father had decorated several of the female mountaineers, informing the representives of the capitalist foreign press who had been invited, 'Here in front of you, you see the pride of Soviet Womanhood. Not only are they

* See *Operation Leningrad* by Leo Kessler (Severn House) for further details.

103

true women –' Stalin had licked his lips, as if he were suddenly very hungry and eyed the enormous bosom of the senior sergeant upon whom he had just pinned the Order of the Red Banner – 'but they are also true patriots, who are prepared every day to sacrifice their very lives in our great patriotic war.' Thereafter, even the old, hard-drinking marshals of the *Stavka* had not dared criticize this unique woman's formation.

They were now camped out in the high mountains of the Caucasus, aware that their opposite numbers, the Fritz, *Gebirgsjäger*, were somewhere down below and advancing in their direction. Mikailovna and her women prepared to meet their enemy. As the Red Eagles clustered around their campfires, warming their rations of soup to be followed with *Kniska* – dried fish – staples of their meagre diet, she decided it was time to brief them. This time, what was to come was not merely a climb followed by an assassination of some unsuspecting Fritzes, who had not realized until it was too late that the Russians were so close. This time the Red Eagles would be opposed by tough mountain men who were probably more skilled than they were: men who had been brought up in the high mountains and who had naturally much more combat experience than this hastily recruited group of female climbers.

'*Tovarischi* – comrades.' She broke into the evening chatter. 'A moment before we sleep.'

They paused, mouths full of black bread and dried fish, some with spoons poised in mid-air.

'Tomorrow we march into the high mountains.' She indicated towards the glistening snow peaks in the far distance. 'If the Fritzes are anywhere, they'll be there. But one word of warning.' She looked at her girls sternly. 'We have never tackled heights like that before. There the peaks are not much less than that of Mount Everest – and we have no oxygen. Not only must we tackle the Fritz expert climbers, but we shall be fighting in the death zone, where people go mad, collapse for lack of oxygen . . .' She let her words trail away to nothing. She didn't want to frighten them, especially the younger ones, who were really mere rock scramblers.

Major Mikailovna need not have feared. Her girls, as she

called them, were not perturbed by her words. One of the senior sergeants, a big, robust woman with ragged, cropped hair and what looked suspiciously like a moustache under her big nose, swallowed her chunk of black bread and cried, 'We'll make it, Comrade Major, come what may. Why, when the Fritzes see us, they will be so taken in by our lovely mugs, they'll fall in love with us – or crap their breeches.' Suddenly she flung up her big clenched fist in the communist salute. '*Slava Krasnaya Armya!*' she cried with all her strength.

'Long live the Red Army.' The women echoed the sergeant's words . . . '*Slava Krasnaya Armya.*'

Round and round that proud slogan raced about the mountains and suddenly the Major felt her eyes flood with tears. What a brave loyal bunch her girls were. Five minutes later the sun had vanished behind the mountains and all was darkness . . .

Three

An owl hooted. A silver moon scudded across the mountain vista.

Icy light shot back and forth across the narrow pass they had to take.

It threw into relief the straw-roofed huts of the tribesmen who had been taking potshots at Sturmer's men all afternoon, as they had climbed down to the rendezvous with Wotan, several kilometres to the west.

Colonel Sturmer shivered in the night cold. It was two o'clock in the morning and since darkness had fallen it had snowed twice: thin bitter flakes of icy snow that penetrated to the very bone and had soaked the waiting mountain troops lying in it. Yet again, Sturmer looked at the green-glowing dial of his wristwatch. He was impatient to be moving into the attack before his poor soldiers froze to the damned ground but he could still hear the occasional sound from the tribesmen's positions above and he forced himself to wait a little longer. He knew from past experience that in the middle of the night the human being's metabolism was at its lowest ebb. That was the best time to attack. But although he had far superior firepower than the natives, they were still in the better position and, even armed as they were with their antiquated rifles that seemed to date from last century, they could inflict casualties; and out here in the wilderness he couldn't afford casualties. What would he do with seriously wounded men? He certainly couldn't leave them behind for the tribesmen to deal with; he knew what their fate would be at the hands of those hooknosed bastards.

He shivered again and remembered Napoleon, just before the *Grande Armee* was to be launched into battle, asking his

Marshal Ney, over breakfast, 'Marshal, are the troops fresh?'
Ney had replied cynically in his normal hardboiled fashion,
'Yes, sire, fresh enough. It's been raining on them most of
the night.' Sturmer smiled momentarily at the thought. With
the snow-rain that his troops had been subjected to since
darkness fell, *his* men would be more than fresh.

The big mountain colonel's plan of attack was simple
enough. While one company, under Greul, advanced slowly,
very slowly up the track to the pass, avoiding casualties if
they could, Sturmer and a small group of volunteers would
fade into the silver night, hoping the exchange of fire on the
path would drown any noise they might make. With luck
they'd be able to flank the tribesmen, take their tumbledown
mountain village and, by setting it on fire, or something of
that nature, force them to retreat into the open. Then, as
Greul had remarked earlier on, eyes blazing with rage at the
affrontry of these 'savages', as he called them, 'they'll learn
that it is not wise to attempt to oppose the might of the
greater German armed forces.'

Sturmer threw another glance at his watch. It was time to
go. He cocked his head to the wind. It bore no sound. He
hoped that meant the tribesmen up above them had finally
gone to sleep. If they hadn't, well, Sturmer shrugged his
shoulders, everyone has to take his chances in this war.

He nudged Ox-Jo. 'We're ready. Signal to Major Greul.
Then we move out.'

Ox-Jo nodded. He cupped his hands around his mouth
and imitated the hoot of the mountain owl which he had
heard a little while before. Greul acted immediately. Cold
and stiff as he might be, Greul was a man who could always
be relied on to carry out an order promptly. From his own
position, Sturmer could hear the faint noise as the men under
the Major's command moved out, the metal parts of their
weapons and equipment wrapped in rags and anything else
they could find to deaden the sound.

Now Sturmer counted the minutes as they passed,
attempting to calculate when the tribesmen would spot the
attackers and begin firing. Then he could start his own part
in the operation. Finally the troops were ready. There was

still no sound of firing from up ahead, but Sturmer knew that Greul's luck couldn't hold for ever. 'Move out,' he commanded hoarsely.

'Thank God,' Ox-Jo moaned, as grumpy as ever, 'Any longer here, sir, and I'd have grown barnacles on my arse.'

Sturmer didn't comment.

Like grey ghosts in single file, Sturmer and his men slipped into the silver shadows and moved almost silently onto the little track, following the fringe of snow as a guideline leading up to the left of the pass. In the lead, Sturmer waited for the first shot, which would indicate Greul's force making the feint up the road. But still all was quiet, save for the harsher breathing of his men as they began the climb. He nodded his approval. The closer they got to the tribesmen holding the path, the easier they'd be able to deal with the enemy at close quarters and, if they were lucky, fight their way through without casualties. He dreaded, as he had since they had started this mission, the thought of casualties. What would he do with a seriously wounded man? He couldn't leave him behind at the mercy of the tribesmen, who knew no mercy. And he couldn't steel himself to put a wounded man out of his misery as the SS did. The very thought of the *Gradenschuse* – the shot of mercy – as the SS officers called the pistol shot to the base of the wounded man's skull was totally abhorrent to him.

Slowly they wound their way up the twisting path, glad of the snow fringes to guide them, for now they were faced by a sheer drop to their left. One wrong move and a man could tumble hundreds of metres to his death.

The minutes passed slowly. They froze as the heavy silence was broken by the sudden howl of a dog above them, followed by a series of angry barks, which ended in an abrupt howl as if someone had just thrown a stone at the animal to silence it.

Behind Sturmer, Ox-Jo growled '*Himmelherrje*, I nearly pissed myself.'

At his side, one of the mountaineers added, 'What d'yer mean, Sarge? *Nearly*! I have pissed meself.' And he meant it.

Despite the tension Sturmer grinned. The men were in good heart, despite the danger. They plodded on.

Up ahead, with his men strung out in files in battle order on both sides of the rough road leading to the pass, Greul was angry. It went against his National Socialist ethic to treat these third-class human beings of tribesmen as serious opponents. Why waste all this time? Rush the sub-humans, he told himself, and have done with it. If they suffered casualties, well, they suffered casualties. After all, it was a soldier's duty to fight, take risks and, if necessary, to die in battle. He moved forward at increased speed, as if he were only too eager to come to grips with the enemy, telling himself the CO was too soft with the men. Indeed, he lacked that arrogant National Socialist spirit which overcame all obstacles, whatever they were.

Behind him, Sturmer was facing a new trial which slowed down his advance. It was a section of steep rock, overgrown with some sort of prickly creepers. Whether the creepers were intended deliberately to protect the mountain village, Sturmer didn't know or care. He was too concerned with getting his men through the barrier without a sound, for the creepers tore at a man's flesh mercilessly. His soldiers were especially vulnerable as they were unable to locate the damned things in the darkness.

Doggedly, with Sturmer still in the lead, they started to work their way through the creepers, making painfully slow progress. Once they nearly tumbled into a ditch concealed by the vegetation; it was filled with *panjes* – pointed stakes set at a sixty degree angle. Anyone who fell on one of them would suffer terrible wounds. Sturmer shivered a little at the thought, visualizing himself dying slowly with a stake skewered through his guts. It was obvious that the creepers and the stakes had been deliberately planted there to protect the village.

A few minutes later he forgot the stakes, as he heard the first single rifle shot, from up on the road, sounding like a dry twig being snapped underfoot in a hot summer. Instinctively Sturmer knew that Greul had been spotted. In the next instant he knew he was right. The high-pitched hiss of a machine pistol could be heard. Someone was replying to that single shot with a Schmeisser. Sturmer cursed. Greul should have waited before opening fire, the defenders of the pass now knew the Germans were there. Behind Sturmer, Ox-Jo expressed it in his own coarse fashion with, 'Now our hooters are right deep in the shit.' And he was right. Almost immediately an angry firefight broke out and, with sinking heart, Sturmer knew they weren't going to force the pass that easily.

Approximately two kilometres away, on the high plateau below the pass, von Dodenburg awoke at once. Instinctively, old hare that he was, he knew that there was trouble in the offing as he became aware of the firing, muted as it was – and there was no mistaking the sound of German weapons being fired. It was Sturmer and his mountain boys all right.

Even before he could sound the alarm Schulze, in charge of the sentries that night, was bellowing urgently. 'Hand off yer cocks, on with yer socks! . . . *alarm . . . alarm!*'

Like the highly trained soldiers they were, the men reacted immediately. Even the greenbeaks who had joined the Wotan before they had left Germany knew what to do. In fact, von Dodenburg wondered if the whole company could have functioned without him as the drivers hopped into the seats of the self-propelled guns; the panzer grenadiers, whose task it was to protect the outer shell of the metal monsters from infantry attack, took up their positions; the drivers already beginning to tune their engines in the pre-dawn cold while the radio operators waited to be ordered to get on the net.

Von Dodenburg, buckled on his pistol belt and, pulling up the collar of his leather jacket against the mountain cold, searched the horizon in the midst of all this controlled confusion, trying to locate exactly where the firing was coming from.

'*Daoben . . . rechts,*' he barked at Schulze, his breath fogging in a grey cloud in the cold air.

'Got it, sir,' Schulze answered, noting the red stabs of angry flame cutting the air on the top of the pass, illuminating the stark black outline of some kind of native village. 'What's the drill?'

Von Dodenburg made a snap decision. 'Give the village a couple of rounds.'

'With the greatest of pleasure, sir. But what about our boys, those Bavarian barnshitters like Matz here.'

Matz opened his mouth to protest. But Schulze was already doubling over the nearest SP, yelling 'Elevation thirty degrees . . . High Explosive . . . target.'

As the gunner whirled his wheels urgently, sweat breaking out on his brow despite the biting cold, von Dodenburg waited impatiently. He could tell by the increasing volume of fire that Sturmer's battalion was having a tough time of it. And they weren't making any progress against whomever was holding them up. The mountain men's fire was not getting closer as it should have done if they were advancing.

'*Feuer frei!*'

Schulze's cry cut into von Dodenburg's thoughts. He didn't hesitate. 'Feuer!' he cried at the top of his voice.

The gun of the self-propelled artillery piece belched. The shell hissed out of the tube. For a moment the air stank of burnt explosive. Then, with a roar like a midnight express speeding through a deserted station, the shell screamed upwards. The next instant it slammed back to the ground again, making the very earth tremble. The battle for the pass had properly commenced.

Kilometres away Major Mikailovna stirred uneasily in her sleeping bag, vaguely aware that something had gone wrong.

111

Four

As the first shells started to fall on the tribesmen's village, the defenders of the pass began to panic. In all probability this was their first experience of shellfire. They streamed down the road from their dug-in positions, stopping Greul's men in their tracks, as they attempted to break through the mountaineers and escape that terrible fire.

Sturmer and his men were in a better position. Yet as Greul tried his best to hold the attackers, who were carried away by their fear, the hook-nosed tribesmen diverted to left and right, hitting Sturmer's men almost at once. Suddenly he and his handful of volunteers, under Ox-Jo, were being assailed from all sides, as the attackers erupted from the foliage yelling crazily, firing from the hip, as they charged down the slope in a flurry of stones, dust and gravel; some of them waving short curved swords – like something out of the middle ages.

What Sturmer had feared most now began to happen. His men started to take casualties. He thrust his way forward, the thorns tearing cruelly at his flesh. Two of the natives came running at him, screaming hysterically at the tops of their voices, swords raised, faces gleaming with sweat in the silver moonlight.

Sturmer fired to left and right without aiming. The one to his right screamed as he went over the side of the cliff. The other skidded to a sudden stop. For what seemed an age, he simply stood there. Sturmer fired again. Nothing happened. Sturmer cursed. He had a stoppage. The man tottered forward. Sturmer's nostrils were assailed by his rancid stench. Sturmer raised his useless weapon butt forward but did not need to use it. The native gave a strange throaty noise that appeared to come from deep down within him. He raised his sword, planning to bring it down and cleave open Sturmer's skull but he was unable to do so. The sword tumbled from his suddenly nerveless fingers and clattered to the rocks. He fell to the ground, dead before he reached it.

Further up the ascent, a party of the frenzied tribesmen had turned upon one Sturmer's mountaineers who had fallen to the ground wounded. Madly they hacked away at the defenceless man. Sturmer fired at them from the hip. Both went down in a confused flailing of arms and legs, blood spurting from their chests, torn apart at such close range. Another injured mountaineer dropped to his knees. As the frenzied tribesmen, panicked by the hollow boom and crash of the self-propelled guns and desperate to get away, saw the man go down, they were on him in a flash. It was as if they thought they had to saw their way through the mountaineers if they were to escape. Again in primitive fury they started hacking and cutting at the defenceless man. Ox-Jo gave a mighty roar, that savage Bavarian temper of his making him forget all danger to himself, and he charged forward. Not for long. He stumbled in a patch of darkness, possibly catching his boot on one of the roots. With a cry of despair, he disappeared from view, the cry following him as he fell into a deep crevice.

Again Sturmer snapped quick unaimed shots to left and right, crouched there like some western gunslinger in one of those *Ami* films that had been popular. At such close range he couldn't miss. One tribesmen went down. Then another. Another came towards him, waving his sword. Sturmer gave him a burst. The tribesman screamed shrilly, stopping midstride, his sword falling from his hand, his stomach ripped apart. What looked like a steaming grey-dull green snake emerged from his abdomen. He wailed and tried to hold his intestines. Sturmer kicked him in the face with his mountain boots and rushed on, springing over the other dead tribesmen to the crevice where Ox-Jo had fallen.

'*Mir nach*,' he gasped.

His men followed. The tribesmen saw them and parted to left and right in their panic-stricken flight from the shells. They didn't want to tackle so many. Sturmer dropped his weapon, safe now, and went on his knees. He peered down the narrow but deep hole in the ground. He could just make out the white blur of Ox-Jo's face some twenty or more metres below. He was lying, unmoving, his massive bulk curled in a kind of foetal position.

Sturmer looked grim as the firing on the other side of the pass started to die away. From the odd moan that Ox-Jo emitted, he guessed he might be badly hurt, but he was at least alive. It would help if Ox-Jo could take orders because it was going to be one hell of a job under the circumstances to bring him up. But it had to be done.

As Greul and the main body pushed onwards to the village and the tribesmen scattered, he forgot the war and concentrated on the rescue, as if this was some peace time climb and he was dealing with an injured team member.

Looking down the crevice and trying to assess the best way to deal with this emergency Sturmer said quietly, 'Rope . . . as much as you can find.'

'Sir,' someone said from the little crowd gathered around, as if in protest.

'At the double,' he cut the man short. 'We haven't much time. I'm going down, as soon as you can find the rope.'

Closing his ears to the angry snap-and-crackle of the small arms battle and cries from up above, Sturmer folded the rope over his shoulder. There was no time for him to rope up; he would have to go down just as he was. Carefully he lowered himself over the side of the narrow crevice. It was a tight fit but he noted, with some relief as he commenced the descent, that the chimney broadened as it went deeper. He thanked God for that. They'd need all the space available if he was to get Ox-Jo's bulk to the surface.

The rock surface was difficult. Despite the permanent coldness of the area, the rock was damp and made even more slippy by the verdigris which had spread over it. It needed all his skill to keep a grip on it; he would usually use his shoulder, to take the strain during a climb of this nature. This time he used his nailed boots on the rock, which had a tendency to slip if he wasn't careful, and which placed more strain on his calf-and-thigh muscles. These burned now, as if someone had thrust red-hot pokers into them. Still he persisted, trying to ignore the pain and at the same time to not hurry. Hurrying could be fatal.

Slowly but surely he began to progress downwards aware of Ox-Jo's low moans, a kind of eerie keening, which indicated he was beginning to come round. He hoped, however, that the hulking NCO wouldn't gain full consciousness before he was ready to get him to the surface. He didn't want his concentration disturbed by Ox-Jo moaning out loud. As the chimney broaded, Sturmer changed his technique several times. Using all his expertise as a veteran climber, he changed between knee-jam, friction hold and press-and-push; his face streaming with sweat, his whole body burning with the strain of it all.

At one point he slipped and hung there by his finger-ends, his face tortured and beetroot red as he swung there momentarily before he could regain his position and continue the descent.

Five minutes later, he reached Ox-Jo who had regained consciousness, though the big man threatened to black out again at any time. He checked Ox-Jo swiftly. His leg was lying at an absurd angle and when Sturmer ran his hand along it and touched the bone that protruded through the torn trouserleg, Ox-Jo yelped with agony. Sturmer cursed. Ox-Jo had broken his leg – that meant trouble.

Ten minutes later, with the sound of firing from above virtually over, they had managed to haul the big NCO to the surface. All the mountaineers were trained in first aid. In climbing – both in peace and war – there were always accidents and the Bavarians had been trained to cope with injuries, especially those involving broken bones. Now they worked on Ox-Jo.

Sturmer waited a while before he headed up to the pass to see what Greul was up to and how many casualties they had suffered. Twice Ox-Jo passed out as they applied a splint to his left leg without the benefit of pain-killing drugs. The broken leg wasn't as bad as Sturmer had first feared. It was just above the ankle; with the aid of the *streckverband** that his men were fixing and the splint, Ox-Jo might be able

---

* A kind of tight, criss-crossed bandage which would keep a small bone in place.

to hobble at least. But he'd be unable to travel any distance, Sturmer reminded himself. He'd be forced to leave the NCO behind.

Ox-Jo, his face ashen and covered with a lather of unhealthy sweat, seemed to realize that; and for the first time since he had known the NCO, Sturmer could see he was afraid. 'Sir,' Ox-Jo quavered, as someone gave him a sip from his water-bottle, 'You're not going to leave me behind, sir? You're not, are you? Those devils'll show no mercy.'

Sturmer jerked involuntarily. For a moment he thought the frightened NCO was going to grab him by the tunic in his panic.

'No, of course not, Sergeant Mayr. Once we've organized the village up there, we'll see you're safe from them.' He hesitated. 'There'll probably be other wounded who will have to be left behind temporarily.'

There were. At Greul's command, a patrol went round the village, shooting the wounded tribesmen who had been unable to flee, and looting the *isbas* of whatever food and drink they contained. As the men shoved out the veiled women and the pot-bellied kids roughly, Sturmer saw his surmise had been correct.

There were about half a dozen wounded men, who it would be impossible to move. The elderly medical sergeant said, with a grim look, 'Two belly shots, sir, and one with a bullet through his lungs. I can't do much with them, sir, but keep them comfortable and free from pain.'

'They can't be moved then?' Sturmer asked, trying to smile at the wounded, already knowing the answer before the sergeant replied.

The medic wiped the blood off his hands on the dirty white apron he had put on to attend the wounded. 'No sir. They wouldn't last long if we tried, even on those mules over there.' He indicated the village's pathetic collection of small mules and *panje* ponies, skinny-ribbed with dropping heads, as if they might fall down dead at any point.

Sturmer forced himself to keep on smiling. He knew wounded soldiers well. In combat they might be the bravest men on earth, but once they had been hit, they usually lost their nerve totally. Abruptly they became a bunch of old women, who had to be spoiled and reassured all the time. A smile from him, Sturmer knew, would reassure them, for a while at least.

Greul thought otherwise. He came round the bend, kicking a child who had the audacity to get in his way, a smoking pistol still in his hand.

His face was dirty, but flushed with triumph and victory. 'We showed the inferior bastards all right, sir. They ran – those who could still do so – like the sub-humans they are.' He licked his parched lips and looked at the wounded, his hand tightening its grip on the butt of his pistol, as if he were prepared to shoot them there and then. '*Klotz am Bein,*'* he said sotto voce. 'Shall we get rid of them?' His query was matter-of-fact, as if he were asking for permission to shoot some looted pig for a battalion celebration.

Hardened as he was to the ways of combat soldiers, brutalized by war, Sturmer was shocked. 'Certainly not!' he barked. 'What are you thinking of, Herr Major?'

Greul seemed puzzled by Sturmer's outburst. 'But they are a burden on us, sir,' he said, as if it was the most obvious thing in the world. 'What use are they to us – in that condition.'

'They are men, *our* men, Greul,' Sturmer retorted angrily, but before he could say any more, there was the rattle of rusty tracks coming up from the other side of the pass. Sturmer knew it had to be von Dodenburg and his armour of SS Assault Regiment Wotan. He dismissed Greul with an angry 'Set up the perimeter defence . . . I'm going to confer with *Hauptsturmführer* von Dodenburg.' And then he was gone – to meet the newcomers and discuss the problem of the wounded.

* Literally 'Clot on the leg', ie a hindrance.

Five

'Well, I'll piss up my sleeve,' Schulze growled, as he spotted Ox-Jo lying with the other wounded men of the mountain battalion. 'It's the Bavarian barnshitter.'

Ox-Jo looked up at the grinning Wotan NCO miserably. 'I've been hurt,' he moaned. 'That's why I'm here.' He indicated the furs with which the village women had been ordered to cover the wounded.

'Oh,' Schulze said airily, 'I thought you was just having a bit of a lie-down. I know you Bavarians are a bit on the frail side.'

Under normal circumstances Ox-Jo would have been at a grinning Schulze's throat with his knife in a flash, but not now. He was one of the wounded. It was the duty of those who weren't to do their best for their less fortunate comrades. 'I'm a bit dry, *Kumpel**,' he said weakly. 'Could you please pass me that gourd over there. It's a sort of drink and medicine.'

Schulze's eyes glinted greedily. 'Medicine, eh,' he echoed, remembering what he'd heard about these native medicines. There was supposed to be more alcohol in them than anything else and where alcohol was concerned 'Frau Schulze's handsome son' was an expert. 'I'd better taste it, hairy arse, just in case it ain't right for you, *Kumpel*.'

He grabbed the gourd, opened it, took a little sip, his eyes glinting even more, and then, without any further hesitation, he took a mighty swig.

Next to him Matz, who could already smell the vodka of whatever the alcohol was contained in the primitive jug, cried, 'Hold hard, arse-with-ears, save some for your friends.'

* pal. *Transl.*

118

Schulze wiped his abruptly red lips slowly and then raising one mighty haunch let rip one of his long, not unmusical, farts that had made him famous throughout the *Waffen SS*'s NCO corps. 'Prima!' he commented. 'I think I'm going to like this job of playing nursery maid to you poor wounded soldiers, yessir.'

The mixed column of Wotan troopers and mountain men riding on the former's self-propelled guns departed on their mission, leaving the two NCOs and one gun, plus the old sergeant-medic, in charge of the wounded and the local women, who had been left in the village at Sturmer's express command. Despite Greul's vehement protests that 'they'll slit the throats of our wounded at the first opportunity, sir. You simply cannot trust these degenerates,' Sturmer had insisted, maintaining, 'We need the women to tend our people. Don't worry, Greul, if I know anything of our men they're more likely to die of other causes –' He made an explicit gesture with his hand and fingers – 'than from women wielding knives.' But, as usual, irony – especially when it had sexual undertones – was wasted on Major Siegfried Greul.

A happy Matz and Schulze got the women working by feeding them *Wehrmacht* cigarettes, the first the women had seen wrapped in proper cigarette paper instead of leaves, encouraging them to work for the very men who had slaughtered their menfolk that same day, while the mixed column ground over the rough road towards the still not visible 'Elbrus Hotel', as they were calling it. As Sturmer and von Dodenburg lay sprawled on the deck of the leading self-propelled gun, enjoying the morning sunshine, Sturmer explained. 'We don't know if the place is occupied. I hope it isn't, but if it is I intend to take it, von Dodenburg, and use it as my base for the ascent. You will naturally help me if we do have to attack.'

Von Dodenburg nodded his understanding, only half-listening. He was entranced by the beauty of the morning and silent majesty of the snow-heavy peaks ahead. He had no personal ambitions to climb mountains, but he could understand their attraction. They seemed so remote from the mundane cares of the average city dweller. They made him forget the war and the responsibilities that had been placed on his young shoulders. Back in 1939 he had never thought he would one day be in charge of the lives of nearly two hundred young men, making decisions on whether they would survive or not. But for the moment, dwarfed into insignificance by the mountains, he forgot even that.

'Will all your men climb with you, sir?' he heard himself asking, watching a pair of hawks circle the thermals, rising higher and higher, ready to pounce. How effortless they seemed.

'No,' Sturmer answered. 'I shall pick four teams of the best climbers. Two of those teams will climb with us from the Hotel Elbrus till we reach the base of what that big sergeant of yours called the "twin tits". There the best two of the four will climb the rest. If one team fails, I hope the other will manage it.

'Then we plant the flag, take some photos of the event for the press at home and then it's back to mother, double-quick speed. I'm not going to linger up there long. Too dangerous. Once the Popov planes spot us, as they probably will—'

Sturmer stopped short. Suddenly, startlingly, the first hawk had fallen out the sky. It swooped down at a terrific rate. It was almost too fast for von Dodenburg and Sturmer to follow. Then when it seemed about to smash into the steppe, it stopped short. An instant later it was screeching up into the hard blue sky with its prey, a small rabbit, wriggling frantically between its cruel claws.

Sturmer shivered slightly.

Von Dodenburg asked, 'Cold sir?'

Sturmer shook his head, 'No a louse must have run over my liver – that's all.' He fell silent and didn't explain. He didn't need to. Von Dodenburg understood. That act of nature seemed to symbolize their lives. One moment everything was beautiful, peaceful, tranquil; the next their world was transformed into something cruel, violent, without mercy . . .

High above them, Sergeant Lermintov of the Red Eagles ignored her stiffness and the cold – she was just above the snowline; perfectly camouflaged in her white snowsuit – and

120

carefully adjusted her binoculars. Expert that she was, she took great care that the lenses didn't reflect in the thin sunshine and betray her position.

The Fritzes were obviously moving according to a plan. They were not taking the usual hesitant precautions of having a vehicle and a squad of infantry ahead while the main body followed at some distance. They clearly knew where they were going and what to expect in front of them. The sergeant with a hard face and roughly cropped hair, frowned puzzled. What was their objective?

There was another piece of the mosaic that puzzled her, too. The fact that they had left a small garrison and an armoured vehicle at the native village some kilometres to their rear. Was it a base camp? Whatever it was, it was clear that the village secured the route; a route that they would return along.

Her frown deepened. She had to come up with some sort of explanation soon. The Comrade Major and the rest of the Red Eagles' battalion were waiting under better cover a kilometre to her rear, and she knew the Major wanted her report soon. As dearly as she loved the Comrade Major, in a female passion that was unrequited, she feared her temper. So what was going on?

It was nature itself which provided the answer to the question that she desperately sought. As she raised her glasses again to scrutinize the column far below, it happened.

The sun brightened a little; it was located a pale, luminous yellow behind the mountains in front in the direction the Fritz column was taking. Abruptly, everything there was illuminated a stark black but there was no mistaking the towering, buttressed giant – Mount Elbrus.

Hastily the Sergeant adjusted her glasses. Yes, it was Elbrus with its twin peaks, all right. She lay there, rigid in the snow, ignoring the cold and her stiffening limbs, entranced not only by the sight, but by her own sense of enlightenment; she was delighted by the fact that she felt she had solved the problem, one which had agitated her ever since she had first spotted the enemy on the mountain road.

Then the mountain was gone, as the shadows swept across

the mountain range once more and the sun weakened. But she continued to lie there, hardly daring to believe that she had solved the problem. An inner voice told her she had. It rasped at the back of her mind, 'You silly old *babushka* – hurry . . . inform the Major at once . . . She *must* know.' She snapped out of her reverie – letting the binoculars drop to her chest. She rolled over and pulled out the yankee walkie-talkie with which the Red Eagles team were equipped, thanks to Comrade Stalin. She ripped up the aerial, hoping that the radio could carry its limited range of five kilometres in the mountains. She gave the call signal dispensing with radio procedure in her haste to inform the Major of what she knew. She began talking so excitedly to the Major that the latter was forced to calm her with 'All right . . . all right, Comrade Sergeant . . . Just start at the beginning again and tell me – *slowly* – what you have found out.'

Sergeant Lermintov, her heart pounding wildly, not only with the excitement of what she now knew, but also with the emotional strain of talking to the woman she loved, the one she felt more for than all those silly young girls that she took to her bunk for sex when she could no longer fight the urge between her sturdy thighs. 'Comrade, the Fritzes have a definite objective. That is clear from what I have seen.'

'*Horosho*,' the Major said. '*Favorit* – speak it.'

The sergeant licked her suddenly parched lips before announcing, 'It's the mountain, Comrade Major.'

At the other end of the line, the Major, surrounded by her waiting headquarters company – all armed and ready to attack – snapped, angry at the veteran sergeant, who seemed to have lost her head and was talking woolly nonsense as if she were afflicted by mountain sickness. 'What mountain, Comrade Sergeant?' she demanded sharply.

'Elbrus . . . Mount Elbrus, Comrade Major . . . The Fritzes are marching on Elbrus.'

PART FOUR
Old Leather Face Makes a Decision

One

The Soviet dictator wasted no time. Once he had received the high priority signal from the Red Eagles' commander, he realized that this was something he could not pretend to have anticipated. Stalin had always propagated the image of being the Little Father of his long-suffering people and a man who knew *everything*.

As he explained to Beria, his crony and fellow Georgian, 'It is absolutely imperative that the Fritzes are stopped. We cannot allow them to get away with it.'

Beria's eyes, hidden behind the pince-nez which made him look like a sinister, degenerate village schoolmaster, glinted. The man, who one day would murder Stalin, said quietly to an excited Stalin, 'Don't worry, Comrade Secretary, the people need never know even if the Fritzes succeed in whatever they're trying on Mount Elbrus. I will ensure that nothing ever gets out.'

'There are the Red Eagles.'

Beria shrugged. 'They can be as easily liquidated as anyone else, Comrade. They will simply disappear and no one, even their relatives, will dare ask any questions.'

Stalin waved his dirty hand in dismissal. 'You can't liquidate all the Fritzes though, even you can't do that. Once that club-footed little bastard of a propaganda minister of theirs, Goebbels, gets his hands on the story, he'll ensure that the whole damned world knows what happened on Mount Elbrus.'

Beria decided he had gone far enough. He changed his approach, as he had done so often in the years he had worked with Old Leather Face. Even when he was blind drunk at those crazy parties that Stalin enjoyed giving for the more prominent members of the *Politburo*, where Stalin had made even senior ministers dance like Cossack yokels, he had watched his tongue. He asked, 'But what exactly do you think the Fritzes are doing up there, Comrade Secretary?'

Stalin took a hasty puff at his stinking old pipe, so excited that he didn't linger over the taste as he usually did. *'Boshe moi*, how should I know?' he exclaimed angrily. 'All I know is that they aren't a reconaissance party for a major Fritz advance through the high Caucasus. How could they use their armour in that kind of terrain? Impossible.' He spat a disgusting stream of yellow muck onto the marble floor. Immediately the hunchbank came forward from the shadows to clean it up. Neither Beria nor Stalin seemed to notice.

'They will do what they intend on the mountain and then retreat. Whatever that is, it must be stopped at all costs.'

'Those women, Comrade Secretary – the Red Eagles?'

'Yes, the Red Eagles must stop them. Regardless of losses.'

Again Beria shrugged carelessly. 'They're only women, comrade,' he said easily. 'What are women for anyway – to bear children for the future of our nation and naturally to be fucked.' Stalin didn't rise to the bait. 'I suggest, if I dare comrade, that we throw a security blanket over the operation. I am sure you will contain the Fritzes, whatever they are up to there in the mountains.' He paused deliberately.

Stalin nodded slowly, calming down a little. 'Yes, I am sure you are right. But continue.'

'Both the Red Eagles and the Fritzes, those who survive to be captured by our glorious Red Army –' Beria gave a little smile in a frightening manner – 'should be liquidated. In other words, I shall ensure that history will never know that this operation ever took place . . .'

Stalin nodded. 'Agreed . . .'

Over a thousand kilometres away, the wounded sergeant Ox-Jo Mayr was not concerned with history on that fine day in the Caucasian village. Instead he was concerned primarily with saving his own skin. Schulze and Matz were at the other side of the tumbledown village organizing the treat they had ordered for the wounded and – naturally – for themselves. Now safely out of the way, they supervised the village women as they pounded raw mutton, stinking of garlic, into a paste. Others baked bread in primitive ovens which they would cover later in layers of wild honey. But even the sweet smell of newly baked bread didn't deflect Ox-Jo from his task, as he sprawled in the morning sun talking to Egon, the eighteen-year-old driver of the Wotan self-propelled gun.

Ox-Jo considered Egon, a tall blond, weedy boy, as the possible means of escape if things went wrong. The boy's hands trembled slightly and he was always cadging cigarettes, which he only half-smoked, throwing them away nervously, only to attempt to cadge another one minutes later. Egon was the SP's driver, the most important member of the four-man crew of the Wotan vehicle.

With this in mind, he tossed over one of his last remaining cigarettes to the weedy boy, saying heartily, 'Go on, lad, have a lung torpedo. They can't do you no harm.'

Naturally the boy fluffed it and let it drop. Ox-Jo grinned encouragingly. 'Get on with it, lad – enjoy yerself.' By way of encouragement, he even threw his last box of matches across.

'Thanks, Sarge,' Egon said. Hastily he lit yet another cigarette with a hand that trembled badly. 'Good of you.' He took a hurried puff. 'I needed that, Sarge.'

'Don't mention it, son. I know what it is – pissing yerself the first time you're at the front. I was shit-scared. The old cancer stick'll steady yer nerves.'

Egon looked at the huge Bavarian with shoulders that gave him his nickname of Ox-Jo. '*You* scared, Sarge?'

'You betcha . . . and I'm scared again now. Just a handful of us up here in the middle of nowhere. I keep thinking they're watching us all the time, up there in the mountains.'

Egon nearly dropped his cigarette. 'Who . . . where . . . watching us?' he quavered.

Ox-Jo tugged at the end of his big nose, removed a dewdrop and neatly slung it into space. 'You don't think them tribesmen have just done a bunk like that and left us with their women-folk, especially when we've got rumpy-pumpy merchants like that Sergeant Schulze, who can't keep his flies closed for more than an hour, do yer? They're watching us all right, just waiting for a chance to take us by surprise and do what they do to people who – er – interfere with their women-folk.' He made a sweeping motion as if he were holding a sharp knife with his big right hand. 'Off just like that!'

Egon dropped the rest of his cigarette and didn't even notice. 'What d'yer mean, Sarge?' he stuttered.

'They'll have it off yer in zero, comma, nothing seconds, lad . . . I mean yer love tool.'

Egon's hands fled to his loins, as if some evil, hook-nosed tribesman was already attempting to emasculate him. 'They wouldn't.'

'They would,' Ox-Jo said resolutely. 'That's their custom. Shitting lot of heathens . . . they don't know the meaning of the word mercy. One swipe with a sharp knife and it's off. If yer don't bleed to death yer'll be a singing falsetto for the rest of yer life.'

'But I ain't even had—'

'It's all right, lad,' Ox-Jo interrupted him sharply realizing that the stupid 'sow-Prussian' was about to break into tears and he couldn't have that. It would be a dead give-away. Then even that big bastard, Schulze, would be able to work out that there was something going on. He lowered his voice, as Schulze and Matz appeared over the hill, with a line of village women behind them, bearing trays of steaming food. 'But there is a way out.'

'What?'

'Yes, we don't need to stay here and wait for the others and risk having our love tools sliced off . . . And . . .' He lowered his voice even more. 'And you, lad, have the means of getting us out of here.' He stopped. The others were within earshot. 'I'll tell yer more after we've scoffed some of that blackie fodder . . .'

Unknown to a scared Egon – and Sergeant Ox-Jo for that matter – the tribesmen had long vanished. They were less concerned about the fate of their womenfolk than the problems they might face with those other women, the Red Eagles, if they didn't leave the mountains after Major Mikailovna had sent a runner to order them to do so. They feared the Red Eagles more than Beria's secret police, the NKVD.

As the Red Eagles crowded round their young commander in the main gallery of a series of caves, which she had selected that morning as her HQ, their trim superbly fit bodies shapeless in their thick wadded snow-jackets and coarse serge mountain pants, all of them knew that they had been placed on 'red alert' on the orders of no less a person than Comrade Stalin himself. They were eager to find out what their mission was, though most of them guessed it was something to do with the German column far below.

The Major saw their eagerness. All the same she was well-trained in Soviet idealogy. The battalion possessed no commissar who would have been responsible for propaganda under normal circumstances: to work the troops up into a patriotic frenzy. So she did it herself and even though she knew this little pep talk was a kind of propaganda, she felt in her heart that it contained the truth.

'Comrades,' she commenced, 'I know we live hard and suffer as much as our male comrades, sometimes perhaps even more. I'd like to give you a rest, but I cannot. The Fatherland calls and the Little Father has made a special appeal to us.'

'*Nyet*, Comrade Major,' some of them protested, 'We need no rest. We follow you gladly, even to the grave.'

Sergeant Lanya Lermintov, the Battalion's chief scout, spat into the dust of the cave's floor like a man and growled, 'We are not destined for the grave, comrades. Not yet at least. The graves will be occupied by the Fritzes when I get my delicate paws on them.' She held up her cracked, callused big hands like steamshovels, and the Red Eagles laughed.

The Major did too. Her girls knew the dangers. Why emphasize them? After all these were not silly peasant housewives with their petty worries. These were the elite, the symbol of the Fatherland's New Woman, free of the domestic silliness of the great majority of the female sex. They knew what was expected of them.

She wasted no more time trying to encourage them to one last great effort. There was no need to do so. 'It is my belief,' she informed them, 'that because the Fritzes are made up of first-class mountain troops, they will be heading for the pass.' With the tip of her fighting knife, she sketched the position in the dust on the cave's floor. '– Here. That pass is dominated by what used to be called – before the war – the Elbrus Hotel and it was used by climbers. From that hotel the whole approach area can be covered.' She paused to let the information sink in. Then she went on, 'It is my plan to leave a small group of our Red Eagles at the pass.'

'How many?' Sergeant Lermintov interjected in her blunt masculine manner.

'Not more than two platoons, Comrade Sergeant. Perhaps twenty-five to thirty comrades in all.'

Lermintov shook her wild, cropped head. 'Too few,' she growled. 'No matter. I volunteer to command the pass group.'

Under other circumstances Major Mikailovna would have smiled. But the situation was too serious and Sergeant Lermintov even more so. She said, 'Thank you, Comrade Sergeant. It's yours.'

'I can pick my own people?' Lermintov flashed a swift glance at Lydia, a pretty young blonde straight from high school – her favourite. The latter blushed and hung her head.

'Yes, you can.'

'*Horoscho* . . . it is done.'

The Major didn't dare to enquire why the tough sergeant had looked like that at the eighteen-year-old, but she could guess. Instead she said, 'I and my group will take over Elbrus House.'

Lermintov grinned and said, 'With all due respect, Comrade Major, you probably won't be needed. When they see me, the Fritzes'll probably get their monthlies.'

That did it. The Red Eagles started giggling like the bunch of silly schoolgirls many had been only a few months before. For most of them, those who survived, it would be the last time they would giggle in their lifetime.

Two

'They call it the dead zone,' Sturmer said, almost to himself. 'All the peaks are over eight thousand metres.' He and von Dodenburg were inside the self-propelled gun. It had grown colder and there they were out of the wind. Besides the sky was darkening and von Dodenburg reasoned there was snow in the offing.

'Dead zone?' he queried, half-interested.

'Yes, because up there you're on your own, with a human body that is not designed to function at such a height. It deteriorates rapidly as you struggle for the summit,' Sturmer answered. 'At that altitude, if you make a mistake and you're on your own, you can only live for a few days at most. More likely, you'll survive only a few hours, von Dodenburg. You feel as if you're suffering from a bad attack of the flu and you're pushing yourself as if you are running a great race. You never get enough sleep and you're shedding weight as if you're in a Turkish bath.' He forced a grin. 'Coming back in one piece is a success . . . getting to the summit is a bonus.'

'But why do it, Colonel?' von Dodenburg asked, as the dark clouds above the pass they were approaching became ever more threatening.

Sturmer sniffed, as if he hesitated to give an answer to that overwhelming question. 'God knows. Even the approach march is usually a misery. You begin to suffer from mountain sickness above a certain height. You worry if you've packed your rucksack correctly, whether you have all the equipment you need. Forget your sunglasses and you're probably almost blind within hours.' He raised his voice. 'Why do it?' he echoed von Dodenburg's original question

131

in an oblique manner. 'Up in Nepal, beyond India, there is one peak I want to conquer in the Himalayas. It's over eight thousand and five hundred metres tall. It's called Kanchenjunga. Before the war, several climbers attempted it and failed.'

Sturmer turned and looked at von Dodenburg directly. There was a kind of desperate longing in his keen blue eyes. 'Von Dodenburg, I'd like to tackle that mountain. If I don't make it, then I'll probably die there – and I'll die there free.'

Von Dodenburg was slightly shocked by the Colonel's disclosure. All the same, he realized that he was dealing with an officer whose life wasn't as taken up by the war as his was. It was a kind of revelation for him and his liking for the mountain colonel grew stronger.

Sturmer laughed suddenly. It was a strange sound. But it broke the spell. Chuckling he said, 'Doubt if I'll ever see Nepal and Kanchenjunga with the way we—'

The rest of his words were muted by the first wave of snow that came over the peaks, instantly, blotting out the landscape with its dense whirling white. Down in the driver's seat, the driver cursed as he faced a white-out which reduced visibility to virtually zero. Instinctively he pulled the two tiller sticks which steered the self-propelled gun and acted as a brake. The 30-ton steel monster reacted badly. It zig-zagged sharply from one side of the rough road to the other. As von Dodenburg dropped into the well of the SP next to the furiously cursing young driver, the vehicle almost went over the side before the driver heaved it back onto the road and stalled the engine doing so. Behind them the other SPs started to pile up, skidding and slithering to a stop in the snow, which was falling from the sky in a white sheet, as if some God on high had ordained that nature should blot out the landscape below.

Then there was no sound save for the hiss of the snow and the steady tick of the SPs' engines behind them. Sturmer looked at von Dodenburg and answered his unspoken question imm-ediately. Von Dodenburg had fought 'General Winter', as the troops called the dreadful Russian winters, often enough, in the past years. He knew that his driver and the others had made a bad mistake. They had stopped on a frozen – or in this case – a snowy height. It was going to be a hell of a job getting the stalled tanks started climbing once more. 'Get your men off the SPs, sir, if you would. We'll lighten their frontal load. They can push and help.'

'*Push*?'

'Yes sir. On this kind of snow, one hand will suffice to move all thirty tons of them. It's as if the surface is greased. You'll see, sir.'

But Sturmer wouldn't. Not then at least. As his mountaineers dropped over the side and prepared to carry out orders, a single shot rang out and a mountain trooper pitched face forward into the white snow. Then came the familiar rat-a-tat of a Soviet tommygun at close quarters. They had bumped straight into a Soviet ambush.

Up above the stalled Germans, and on both sides of the steep ascent, the Red Eagles ceased firing and waited for the Fritzes' reaction. Sergeant Lermintov peered through the pelting snow, a hard grin on her bitter face. She could see little in the white-out but she could hear the snarl and rasp of engines, in low gear, as the Fritz drivers tried to start moving upwards in their self-propelled guns. It told her all she wanted to know. For the time being, the Fritzes wouldn't be able to use their armour; and even if they opened fire with their 75mm cannons, her Eagles were dug well enough into the rocks not to suffer too many casualties.

Abruptly there was a break in the snow, and she saw tiny black figures against the snow, slipping in and out of the great boulders which littered both sides of the mountain road. She cursed. The Fritzes were reacting as quickly as they always did in action. Damn them. Still she was confident they didn't present a threat at the moment. The Eagles were holding their fire, to avoid giving their positions away. She'd let the Fritzes come closer before she ordered them to 'open fire'. That'd stop the Fritzes, she was confident of that.

She reckoned she had time to see how Lydia, her friend, was getting on. Lydia had slipped, sneaking into position, and had hurt her foot. They had carried her to the shelter of two great rocks, which acted as a kind of cave and covered her with their blankets. Lermintov pushed back the blanket which protected the make-shift cave from the flying snow and said, 'It's me . . . I've brought you a *pappiroki*, a real one.' Kneeling, she lit the long cigarette with its paper mouthpiece, puffed out a stream of blue smoke, enjoying the sensation for a moment before placing it in the pretty young Eagle's mouth, her other hand falling instinctively on Lydia's ample left breast.

She knew it wasn't the time and place for such matters, but Sergeant Lermintov couldn't help it. Even in the battle the sexual urge couldn't be constrained. Lydia didn't seem to mind. She pressed her own hand on top of the sergeant and the latter could feel the girl's nipple grow and harden with sexual desire.

The hard-faced sergeant with the ragged, cropped hair licked her lips which suddenly felt parched and she knew that feeling was not caused by the new snow. 'You mustn't . . .' she stuttered, in a voice she hardly recognized as her own. '*Nyet.*'

Lydia pressd her hand even harder. She'd forgotten the pain in her foot. She also licked her lips, they turned a startling red. 'Kiss me, please,' she pleaded. 'I want you to . . . *palshalsta.*'

Sergeant Lermintov couldn't restrain herself any longer. She bent and kissed the girl, her tongue penetrating her soft lips and entering Lydia's mouth greedily. Lydia's stomach rose involuntarily as if seeking to be even closer to her lover. Lermintov put her big rough hand between Lydia's now open legs. She knew she couldn't achieve anything there; the girl was too well packed in thick winter clothing. But she had to do it. Lydia moaned again, the cigarette slipped to the floor of the cave, smoking away. The lovers were locked passionately in each other's arms, the war and the Fritzes below forgotten.

Greul paused. His big shoulders covered with snow, he waved his pistol at the little group of volunteers to stop. He bent and sniffed the air. There was no mistaking it. The stink of that filthy coarse black tobacco – the *mahorka*, the Ivans smoked – was in the air. But where was the stink coming from?

While Sturmer had sent a platoon up the road to attack the unseen Russians blocking their advance, Greul had taken it upon himself to recce the right flank with just six volunteers. As he had told them before they had set out on the dangerous mission. 'They are only sub-humans remember, men. They'll run as soon as they see us.'

Ahead of the platoon and knowing that he had not yet been spotted, Greul was prepared to act in his usual brutal decisive manner, which he thought was expected of a German officer; at least by one who believed one hundred per cent in National Socialism and the New Order. Using hand signals, he indicated that his volunteers should advance to left and right of the spot from which he thought the stink of black tobacco came from. Any sound they made was drowned by the relentless hiss of the falling snow. The men crept forward led by Greul.

Sergeant Lermintov couldn't stop herself. She had forgotten the danger and her duty to the Major altogether. Carried away by an unreasoning passion, she kissed Lydia passionately. It was the same with the young girl. She, too, forgot about everything, even the pain in her legs and responded to Sergeant Lermintov's kisses with total abandonment, pressing her body against the sergeant's, the two of them molten together in the all-consuming fire of sex.

It was thus that Greul saw them, as he carefully pulled the blanket that protected the entrance to the makeshift cave to one side. His thin cruel lips curled in contempt and disgust. He had read about such things, but he didn't think they happened in real life: two women hugging and kissing each other, as if they were a man and women. Such decadent and perverted creatures deserved to die. He raised his pistol.

Sergeant Lermintov heard the faint click as the major snapped off his safety catch too late. She turned. Greul fired. At that range he couldn't miss. The sergeant seemed to leap out of Lydia's arms, as if propelled by a gigantic invisible fist. A large patch of blood spread across the white of her camouflaged suit. She fought death in vain. Meaningless sounds came from her shattered throat and then she slumped across Lydia – dead.

Lydia screamed and tried to raise the dead NCO from her body. She couldn't. Greul didn't give her a chance to exert her strength. '*NOW,*' he yelled, carried away by a sudden fury and hatred that he couldn't analyse himself. He pressed his trigger once more. Lydia's face disappeared in a welter of red gore and shining white cracked bone, as if someone had hit a lightly boiled egg with a heavy spoon.

Greul wasted no more time. 'Corporal,' he shouted to the NCO, who gaped open-mouthed at the two women clasped in each other's arms in death, as if he couldn't believe his own eyes. 'Fire the all clear signal . . . Come on, man, move it!'

The corporal 'moved it'. Clambering up to the top of the rock, the snowflakes howling all about him, he pulled the trigger of his signal pistol. *Plop!* A sudden hush. A moment later the green signal flare expoded into a burst of garish green light above the pass, penetrating even the snow storm with its glare.

Sturmer didn't hesitate. He guessed it must be Greul. No one else would have taken the risk of attacking with so few men. He gave two shrill blasts on his whistle. Behind him, an angry von Dodenburg cursed as his armour still stubbornly refused to take the slope and move upwards to the charging mountaineers.

Three

The snow storm stopped almost as suddenly as it had started. The intensity of the flakes decreased and the visibility improved so that von Dodenburg, still trying to get his SPs up the slippery slope, could see the white snow-suited Russians, who had attempted to hold them, slipping back into the mountains, dragging their wounded with them. Half-heartedly, he ordered his gunners to open fire to speed them on their way. It was about all he could do to help Sturmer's mountain troops who were swarming forward expertly to take over the positions being evacuated by the fleeing Russians.

Sturmer nodded to von Dodenburg, wiping the last of the snowflakes from his anxious face. 'So much for modern mechanized warfare, *Hauptsturmbannführer*,' he remarked, indicating a Wotan trooper who was pushing a sliding and skidding self-propelled gun from the edge of the cliff with one hand. 'We've not got that kind of a problem – just two aching feet.'

Von Dodenburg relaxed a little. 'I'd rather ride, *Herr Oberstleutnant*,' he commented.

Together they plodded through the snow to where a triumphant Greul and his handful of volunteers were waiting for them. They passed a dead Russian sprawled face forward in the snow in a star of his own blood. For a Popov, von Dodenburg thought, he seemed to have a lot of hair. But he didn't remark upon the matter.

Greul touched his gloved hand to his peaked cap in a salute. Von Dodenburg and Sturmer responded, but Greul didn't wait for permission to carry on; he was too full of himself and what he had just discovered. '*Meine Herren . . . meine Herren*!' he exclaimed excitedly. 'Will you please look at this.' Without waiting for them to agree, he turned sharply and stalked a few paces through the snow to what looked like a makeshift cave. He flung back the blanket which draped its entrance dramatically and said, 'Look at what these sub-human swine were up to when we surprised them . . . More importantly, gentleman, it shows that the Russian opposition is really quite pitiful.' He paused and waited for their reaction.

Neither of the two other officers were impressed. Sturmer was shocked at the sight of the two dead women slumped over each other, the one beneath with a small breast exposed was a young woman. Von Dodenburg, the veteran, had seen it before. He knew that the average Russian woman in uniform was as tough and as hard – perhaps even more so – than her male equivalent. He remarked drily. 'I hope, Herr Major, that you – we – don't meet many more of that kind.'

Sturmer quickly dismissed Greul's excited discovery with a wave of his hand and the two officers climbed up to the pass, while the gunners threw a shell every thirty seconds over their heads, harassing the fleeing Red Eagles. To the left and right as they moved up they saw the dead women sprawled out in the extravagant, abandoned poses of those done violently to death. Sturmer's mind was too full of what was to come to remark on the dead women, though he did notice that they were fully equipped mountain troops. The women were not just a hastily raised battalion of female auxiliaries to make up for the Red Army's enormous losses; these were obviously highly trained personnel.

The pair paused at the top of the pass and surveyed the front with their field glasses. Dotted in the snowscape were black smoking rings where von Dodenburg's shells had fallen, but otherwise the vast snow plain seemed empty. The women had disappeared, as if they had never even existed. The two officers knew they were there somewhere, but even as Colonel Sturmer remarked upon the matter, von Dodenburg knew that there was little that he and the men of Wotan could do to help him from now on. The terrain was too barren and the climbs too steep for his SPs to function there.

Sturmer knew that, too. For now he had spotted his first objective before they commenced the climb of Mount Elbrus itself. Like a gigantic metallic Pullman car, Elbrus Hotel had emerged from the dying snowstorm to their front. As Sturmer adjusted his glasses to gain more detail he noted that, judging from the melted snow at the strange building's base, it must be occupied. The melted snow indicated that the hotel was being heated; and it was heated because it was occupied. 'Von Dodenburg,' he asked, 'if your SPs could reach the top of the pass, do you think they could range in on that building?'

Von Dodenburg shook his head. 'Even if they could make it under present conditions, I doubt they could be very effective in giving you supporting fire in an attack.' He had already guessed what Sturmer was thinking. 'I don't think we've got the range.'

Sturmer lowered his glasses slowly. 'Well, then young man,' he said, 'I suppose this is where we part company for the time being, eh.' He smiled ruefully. 'It'll be up to us stubble-hoppers, the poor bold hairy-assed Bavarian footsloggers.'

Von Dodenburg smiled too. 'Yessir. Poor old Bavarian footsloggers.'

Sturmer took up his field glasses again and surveyed the building more carefully. It was a long low building, perhaps three storeys high at most, made of a heavy grey stone. This was covered by what looked like duraluminum, as a protection against the winter storms which were horrific at the height of winter. On Elbrus house's flat roof, radio aerials swung back and forth in the wind like silver whips, confirming German Intelligence's belief that Elbrus Hotel had also been used as a weather station before the war.

Sturmer frowned. Again he objected to what man had done to nature. The material to build the damned ugly place had been brought up on the backs of men and animals and dumped. Around the base of the Elbrus Hotel, he could see discarded bricks, and building materials, a great heap of coke, obviously used to heat the building. To Sturmer, the purist, it was just another example of man's persistent efforts to force nature to his will.

Von Dodenburg, a more practical man, filled with the arrogant urgency and dash of the *Waffen SS*, said, as he slung his machine pistol more comfortably over his shoulder, 'A difficult place to attack, sir . . . look at those radio aerials.

It might well be that whoever's holding the place could summon help or supplies by air. A handful of determined men or women could hold out there for days.'

Sturmer didn't seem to hear. Von Dodenburg shrugged and held out his hand. 'Sir, I shall return to the village and form a power base there. As soon as you have accomplished your mission and pull back, we'll be waiting for you there to ensure you are brought back safely.'

Sturmer took the young SS officer's hand and pressed it in his iron grip. Although they came from different worlds and were divided by their different beliefs, he had come to like von Dodenburg. 'Thank you, *Hauptsturmbannführer*,' he said heartily. 'I would appreciate your help.'

Von Dodenburg heard himself say, 'One day, sir, when all this is over and there's peace again, you'll be able to climb that eight thousand metres of yours – Kanchenjunga, isn't it, sir?'

'Yes, that's it. Yes, it's a nice thought, isn't it? Something to look forward to.'

They stood there awkwardly. Then Sturmer took his whistle out of his top pocket and blew a sharp blast on it. It was the signal for his men to assemble and begin the march on Elbrus Hotel.

Von Dodenburg waited as they gathered. The mountaineers lined up in two long files, weighed down with their equipment like pack animals, and trudged over the pass, heading for what lay in front of them. At the top, Sturmer clicked to attention and saluted each troop solemnly as it passed. When they had all gone he, too, turned and vanished over the other side.

Von Dodenburg stood there transfixed, listening to the stomp of the mountaineers' feet in the snow till that sound vanished too. It was only then that he started to make his way back to the SPs at the bottom of the hill; the engines beating slowly, like some monster which had given up in despair in its effort to climb the snowbound ascent. Somehow, he told himself, he couldn't believe he'd see Colonel Sturmer again. The big mountaineer's dream of a kind of peace that would allow him to climb that mountain in far-off Nepal would never be realized. His fate – all of their fates – would be decided in this damned accursed wasteland that was Russia.

PART FIVE
The End Run

One

Noiselessly the fog swept in. Milky-white, like a soft cunning Siamese cat, it curled itself around the house on the height and rested itself there. Within seconds, the fog had virtually obscured the gleaming three-storey building. However, at such a close distance Greul and Sturmer, lying in the snow feeling the warmth of the new warm front on their backs after the cold of the blizzard, could see enough of the building which barred their way to their objective, Mount Elbrus.

Some way behind them their troops had abandoned their heavy rucksacks gratefully and had begun digging almost immediately. They needed no urging. The Popovs held the hotel and might well have some form of artillery – perhaps mortars, and they didn't want to take any unnecessary risks. Even if they were only wounded out here in this remote snowy waste, it was almost a sentence of death. Their officers would have to abandon them. So they dug despite their weariness.

Sturmer lowered his glasses, his eyes a little tired and red-rimmed from the approach march, and said, 'Well, it's defended all right, Greul. You can see the machine guns on the second floor and for all I know they might well have mined the immediate vicinity. They're a tough bunch those women of theirs.'

Greul sniffed in his usual contemptuous manner. 'After all, sir, they are Russian sub-humans – *and women* . . . I don't think they should present much of problem for us. Give me permission, sir, and I'll soon clear the perverted Red bitches out of the place.'

Sturmer made up his mind. He put his glasses back in

their case. 'I have no doubt you would, Greul,' he said easily. 'Unfortunately you'd lose too many good men doing so. Remember, in order to attack a defensive position you need to outnumber the defenders by three to one.'

'But we are German—'

Sturmer cut Greul's protest short. 'I'm not discussing it, Major,' he snapped, 'I'm ordering you. We shall contain the hotel and head straight for our objective, the peak of Mount Elbrus.'

Sturmer took off his glove and fumbled awkwardly in his smock for a ten pfennig piece. 'Let's do it old style, Greul,' he said, forcing a smile. 'We'll toss for the honour of climbing the peak.'

Greul hesitated. He glared at the little brass coin, as if it were some deadly enemy. It would, if he agreed, determine whether he added another peak to his list of conquests. Should he take that risk? Finally he blustered, 'With all due respect, sir, I must register an official protest.'

Sturmer took the statement calmly. 'Register as much as you wish, Major. But this is the way it's going to be.' He balanced the little coin on his thumb and the crook of his forefinger. 'Ready?'

Grumpily Greul echoed, 'Ready.'

'Head or eagle?' Sturmer asked. 'Eagle,' Greul replied.

Sturmer spun the coin and caught it a little clumsily with his stiff fingers. He held it out for Greul to see. 'Head, you stay behind.'

'Damn—' Greul caught himself just in time. A good National Socialist shouldn't give way to his feelings. Still the rage flamed up within him and almost burst through. 'Then you must tackle Elbrus, sir,' he managed to say.

'Yes, you stay behind and contain the hotel, guard our line so we can retreat once we have done what we have come here to do.'

Reluctantly, Greul took the flag from his rucksack. He had volunteered to bring it all this way in the hope that he would be the one to unfurl it on the top of Elbrus – to proclaim to the world that National Socialism had not only conquered the Soviet mountain but also Europe. For him it would be a symbol of the Germanic New Order which had cleansed an old and decadent continent and removed the threat of the Jewish-Bolshevik plague for ever. Now he was to be deprived of that great triumph, which he believed passionately was worth dying for. 'You will take the flag, sir?' he forced himself to say.

Sturmer hesitated.

'The world must know, sir,' Greul said, 'that National Socialism can even triumph over nature itself.'

Sturmer gave in. 'Yes, I'll take the flag.'

Greul gave a thin smile. In his heart he thought that Colonel Sturmer was not worthy of carrying the Führer's sacred blood-red banner with him. 'Colonel, I wish you every success.'

Sturmer nodded. 'Thank you, Greul. I will leave with my teams in ten minutes. *Berg Heil**.'

'*Berg Heil*.'

They left exactly on time, with Colonel Sturmer taking the lead. They had left Greul, who was beginning to hatch a plan of his own, frustration and rage eating at his heart like a powerful corrosive acid.

Despite the fog, the observers on the roof of the hotel made note of the Germans' departure. As the figures plodded steadily towards them through the knee-deep snow, they sent out the agreed signal. 'Fritz on the way . . . Prepare for kill . . . Long Live Mother Russia . . .'

But Sturmer did not know that as he and his men disappeared into the fog. It was zero eight hundred hours. They had the whole day in front of them. It was one thousand and five hundred metres to the top of the western summit of Mount Elbrus.

'*Heaven, arse and cloudburst*'. Sergeant Schulze cursed angrily, his broad face flushed beetroot red, 'What in three devils' name is going on, *Sturmmann*?'

Egon, the callow young SP driver, flushed too, but with guilt. He lowered the jerrican with which he was filling up the fuel tank of the armoured vehicle. 'Nothing, Sergeant,' he quavered hesitantly.

* Greeting used by German mountaineers

'What d'yer mean nothing, you fart in a trance?' Schulze cried as Ox-Jo watched sullenly from the entrance of one of the *isbas*. 'What are you doing using fuel without my permission? You're not going for a little drive in the country, *Sturmmann*, are you? Perhaps stopping in some tavern to drink a glass of beer and scoff a couple of sausages.'

Irony was wasted on the young driver. A little desperately, Egon flashed a glance at Ox-Jo.

'Well?' Schulze demanded, 'piss or get off the pot. What's going on?'

'I'll tell you, *du Saupreuss*,' Ox-Jo snarled.

Schulze swung round on the NCO. As if by magic a pistol had appeared in the latter's hamlike fist. Schulze didn't blink an eyelid. 'Who asked you to open yer trap?' he said, ignoring the pistol.

Behind him Matz whispered, 'Watch him, Schulzi. Remember he's a Bavarian from the high mountains. Those yokels from up there shoot each other for who pays for the suds.'

Schulze ignored his old running mate's advice. 'Well?' he demanded.

Ox-Jo stared back at him defiantly. 'We're doing a bunk, that's what we're doing. Whether you like it or not, we're getting out of here as soon as we're ready and the lad has filled up his tanks. We're abandoned here and I, for one, am not one frigging bit interested in dying for Folk, Fatherland and Führer.' He spat contemptuously into the dirty snow in front of the hut. 'If you heroes of the SS want to die, that's up to you.'

Schulze was caught completely off guard momentarily. He gasped, 'And what about your comrades, the other Bavarian barnshitters? What about them? Who's gonna guard the line of withdrawal?'

Ox-Jo sneered. 'In this war, you sow-Prussian, it's everybody for hisself. I thought even a wooden head like you would have realized that by now. Don't you be getting in my frigging way. We're off and there's nothing you can frigging well do about it. *Manner*!' He raised his voice suddenly.

Ox-Jo sprang another surprise on Schulze. From the other huts the lightly wounded soldiers of the mountain troops appeared, their carbines already raised, fingers resting on the weapons' triggers. There was no doubt about the determination on their hard Bavarian faces. They'd shoot if Ox-Jo ordered them to. All of them were obviously motivated by the fear of being left behind in this mountain wilderness, at the mercy of the Popovs and the savage tribesmen.

'You won't get away with it,' Schulze heard himself say as he felt the cold metallic hardness of a knife being thrust into his hands from behind by Matz. 'Somewhere along the line the chaindogs* will stop you. How are yer gonna explain to those suspicious bastards? No orders, no—'

'I'll worry about that when the time comes,' Ox-Jo replied carelessly. 'If I was you you big streak of northern piss, I'd worry—' The Bavarian never finished his sentence.

With surprising speed for such a big bulky man, Schulze dived forward. He caught Ox-Jo completely by surprise. Ox-Jo jerked up his pistol. Too late! Schulze's knife flashed. With all his strength, he plunged it into Ox-Jo's chest as he sat there on the ground. The Bavarian screamed. High and hysterical like a woman. The blood spurted from the wound in a bright-red arc and the pistol tumbled from his nerveless fingers. '*Don't!*' he pleaded. 'Please, do—'

Schulze showed no mercy, savagely he plunged the blood-red blade into the dying man's chest once again.

Ox-Jo's spine arched like a taut bow. 'Arr.' Ox-Jo uttered a cry that seemed to come from deep within his pain-racked frame. He fell to one side dead.

They stood there frozen, like actors at the end of the third act of some cheap melodrama: the petrified mountaineers staring at their dead leader. Schulze motionless, his great chest heaving as if he had just run a great race, the bright red blood from his knife dripping onto the dirty snow; Egon, the traitor, rocking back and forth and crooning a kind of lament, the saliva dribbling down his weak chin.

The only movement came from Matz. Silently, his dark

*_Wehrmacht_ military police, so-called due to the silver chains of office they wore around their necks. _Transl._

147

eyes watching for any suspicious movement from his fellow Bavarians, he unslung the Schmeisser from his back. He clicked off the safety catch and pulled the bolt back and forth. Even the metallic noise of the machine pistol being cocked for action didn't seem to disturb the eerie, brooding silence. Matz's next words did. Harshly, he snarled, '*Los. Waffen runter*. Drop your weapons . . . at the double quick. *Dalli, dalli.*'

The mountaineers jerked like men coming awake from a deep sleep. One by one, staring at the SS Corporal as if they didn't quite believe that this was happening to them, they dropped their carbines to the ground, while Schulze, also shaking off his trance-like state, bent and wiped the bloody blade of the knife on the dead man's tunic.

This was how von Dodenburg found them some five or ten minutes later. They had not yet recovered from the shock of Schulze's slaughter of the big Bavarian, who had already started to stiffen in the cold mountain air. The Bavarians stood in line in front of the *isbas*, guarded by Matz and his Schmeisser, hands still raised in the air in surrender.

Von Dodenburg needed Schulze's hasty explanation and the sight of a bent-shouldered Egon, sobbing his heart out like a child, to understand what had happened. He stood in the turret of the SP, its engine still ticking over like a metallic heart, his face suddenly bitter and pale. It wasn't the first time he had encountered frightened German soldiers in Russia who had fled the enemy, even tossing away their weapons in their haste to escape the Red hordes. But they had been third-rate stubble-hoppers and rear echelon stallions, as the men of the supply services were called contemptuously by the SS elite. However, these men were the pick of the German army: Sturmer's mountaineers, Egon, one of his own SS men, and probably the crew of the SP too.

At that moment von Dodenburg felt almost sick. If the elite broke and ran, what could one expect from the rest of the rank-and-file of the German *Wehrmacht*? Where was Germany heading if a third-rate country with a large, but untrained and unskilled army, could beat her? What had become of the German army which had conquered the whole of Europe from the Channel to the Urals: an army which was currently taking time out of this damned total war to plant the flag of the New Order on Russia's highest mountain?

It was a thought that von Dodenburg did not want to think to its conclusion. Crises were there to be mastered, and in this case, there was only one way to stop the rot. He pulled out his pistol. '*Sturmmann,*' he addressed the broken young SS driver harshly. 'Stand up straight. Show pride in yourself as a member of SS Assault Regiment Wotan!'

His command seemed to penetrate the consciousness of the sobbing young man. He ceased crying. With a hand that trembled slightly, he pushed back the boyish lock of long blond hair that had fallen over his face. He straightened up. 'Sir?' he said a little weakly.

'*Sturmmann*, you have betrayed your comrades. Have you anything to say?'

Egon swallowed hard, but he managed to speak. 'No sir,' he answered, supporting himself a little against the front of his SP. 'I am sorry that—'

'Then I find you guilty of attempted desertion in the face of the enemy. *Heil Hitler*!' He fired. Egon yelled. The chest of his black tank uniform flushed an instant dull red. He fell to the ground, his face set and hard. His cap, with its tarnished skull-and-crossbones badge, set at a rakish angle. Von Dodenburg strode over to the boy; he didn't check whether Egon was dead or not. Instead he placed the muzzle of his still smoking pistol to the base of the traitor's head. His knuckles whitened around the trigger for a brief instant. He fired and blew the back of Egon's head off.

Two

Sturmer and his small group of chosen men were making excellent progress on the ascent. The initial rock face was broken. Still it offered good hand holds. There were also several very convenient stances where they were able to scramble up quite speedily. Sturmer was pleased. Indeed he had almost forgotten the war and his mission and was enjoying the climb, as if it was peacetime. All the same, the odd rock formations and deep crevices, filled with hard snow, below the snow mounds made it difficult to see any direct route to the summit as they blocked the view upwards.

By midday, he and his little team had covered a good five hundred metres and were advancing upwards quickly. Although he was worried about time, Sturmer still hoped they might make the ascent before it grew dark and avoid having to camp out on the mountain that night.

'Come on, boys.' He kept on cheering his men upwards, knowing that although he was older, he was in better physical shape than many of the younger men. 'We're doing it . . . keep it up.'

Sturmer's euphoria at the challenge of the climb vanished exactly one hour later. Suddenly and totally unexpectedly, they ran into a sheer rock face. Sturmer stopped immediately. It was something he and the less experienced men could not tackle just like that. A little angrily, he surveyed the rock features through his glasses. He frowned. As far as he could make out there were neither handholds nor stance in the next stage of the ascent. Reluctantly he ordered, 'All right, men. Take a break.'

His men needed no urging. They slumped down in the hard frozen snow, grateful for the rest. Stiff as they were

150

with the cold at that height, especially in the shadows away from the warming rays of the sun, they were relieved to stop and hungrily pulled out their rations of hard salami and started to chew at the stiff, if spicy meat. Tired as they were, their eyes were still excited and their conversation animated. Watching them, Sturmer told himself that they were also carried away by the excitement of the mission, the euphoria of tackling this – as far as he knew – unconquered Russian mountain.

He turned to study the mountain face once again. The traverse was, he concluded, one of the worse he had ever seen in his long career in the high mountains. The rock was weathered, wherever it poked through the snow. Moreover it was flaky and clearly unsound in several spots. Still, he thought, they'd manage it. Besides, secretly, he was excited by the challenge it presented to himself but naturally it wouldn't do to tell his young soldiers that.

'Well,' he finally announced, 'it's not best traverse I've seen in my life, men. But I am sure we – you – can manage it.'

His men looked up, their mouths still bulging with sausage and the rock-hard army bread – which packed, as it was, in tin foil, lasted for months.

'*Jawohl*,' a corporal responded. 'As long as we get the lead out of our arses and get on with it.' He giggled suddenly. Nobody seemed to take the fact he had done so to be in any way strange. Nor did anyone remark about the strange unnatural gleam in his bloodshot eyes.

They continued the climb. Naturally Sturmer took the lead. To the right, the ice of ages glittered in the fissures. The troop all fell grimly silent and watchful as they began the traverse. Carefully Sturmer proceeded, centimetre by centimetre seeking blindly with his fingers any slight handhold he could find. His footholds could give at any time and send him plunging to his death in the valley below for he was working his way forward without a rope; but this didn't worry him. Sturmer was an old hand and had long learned to take precautions, but also not to worry overly about the possibility of sudden death. Once he did slip, as a foothold gave way abruptly, but he saved himself in a light-ening switch as he threw his weight onto his other foot and avoided falling. And it didn't affect him – this narrow escape from doom. The fact that another of his men had also started giggling for no apparent reason did concern him. Yet he dismissed the matter and concentrated on the task at hand. The climb continued . . .

Back at Elbrus House, Greul had had enough. The thought that a man like Sturmer, who did not believe in the New Order and the divine mission of National Socialist Germany, was carrying the Führer's banner and would be honoured for it if he succeeded, riled him beyond measure. More impor-tantly, here he was, a faithful follower of Adolf Hitler, being relegated to this subordinate holding mission. What honour could he expect? None.

Then an idea came to him complete and whole, as if in a vision. As a true, loyal subordinate, he must carry out his mission of 'containing' the hotel and its defenders but at the same time he could give himself a chance to have a crack at conquering the peak. As he crouched in the frozen snow, he thought of ascending Mount Elbrus with a kind of almost sexual longing. His loins seemed to ache as if he were about to take a naked woman, thrust himself into her and make her squeal with pain and pleasure. He licked his suddenly dry lips. Why shouldn't he try? He had much more right to the conquest of that peak than Sturmer, the disbeliever, did.

He made up his mind. He would 'contain' the hotel all right but in his own way. By force. The defenders wouldn't expect anyone to be so foolhardy as to attack such a first-class defensive position. He knew the Russians; they were a lazy lot of drunken swine, who always took the line of least resistance unless their political commissars, the *politruks* stood behind them, armed with their tommyguns, forcing them to be alert.

Swiftly he outlined his plan of attack. The men weren't enthusiastic. They showed it. What did that matter to him? Greul asked himself. If they were doomed to die, so be it. They would die for Germany. He waved his machine pistol at them. 'Come on, you dogs,' he snarled contemptuously

'Do you want to live for ever? *Mir nach*!' Without waiting to see if they followed him, he advanced.

In battle formation, the mountain troopers moved to the left and right of the hotel entrance; each man crouched low like countrymen advancing against a heavy rainstorm after a long day in the fields. They came nearer and nearer. The lingering traces of that early milk-white fog still covering them. On and on they came, the men hardly daring to breathe, waiting for that first rippling noise like a stick being run along a set of iron railings. But none came. The place was so quiet it might well have been long deserted, as far as they were concerned at that moment.

Greul, taking the lead, knew it wasn't. He could smell that typical Popov odour, a mixture of black tobacco, garlic and human misery – and something else which might have been the scent of woman.

He wrinkled his nose at the smell. Still he kept his machine pistol tucked close to his right hip, ready to open fire at the first sign of trouble.

Over to his left, the NCO in charge of that flank pumped his clenched fist up and down rapidly three times. It was the infantry signal for advance – at the double. The sergeant had got his men into position and was prepared – his own flank ready to cover fire. Greul signalled 'agreed' and took a deep breath. This was it. He hesitated no longer.

'*At the double*!' he yelled, plunging forward, skidding a little on the frozen snow. Behind him, his men, now carried away by the crazy unreasoning blood lust of battle, yelled wildly and ran after him. Greul fired a burst at the big door. It flew open. Behind him, the nearest trooper lobbed a stick grenade. Greul ducked. Shrapnel flew everywhere. The blast lashed his uniform about his lean body. It took the very air from his lungs but he didn't stop. He sprang up the stairs and fired two quick bursts to left and right. A scream. A bullet-riddled figure in the earth-coloured smock of the Red Army slumped in the corner. Even as he dashed by her, Greul could see from her bulging bosom that the dying enemy was a woman. The fact didn't worry him one bit. 'Secure the entrance!' he yelled above the chatter of an old-fashioned

153

Soviet machine gun which had begun firing. 'Grenades!'

His men began lobbing grenades to their front. It was the usual tactic. A dangerous one. But some of them were old hares. They knew the technique: throw, duck, advance. Those who didn't duck in time – well it was just too bad. As the old hares were wont to say, 'Well, at least try to make a handsome corpse, comrades.'

The covering barrage worked though. Slowly and doggedly the men in the lead advanced up the broad stairs, now filled with dead and dying Red Eagles, while outside the flank guard, under the command of the NCO, sprayed the upper storeys with interdicting fire, waiting for their turn to enter.

Up in the third storey, Major Mikailovna realised that they were losing control and that she was the cause of it. She had weakened her Red Eagles by dividing their strength between the Fritz armoured force on the road and here, where she had hoped to stop their mountain infantry. It seemed she had failed to do both. The armoured force returning to the mountain village was still intact and it was clear that some of the Fritz infantry had slipped by her in the direction of Mount Elbrus. She was no longer capable of holding the hotel base under such a determined and ferocious Fritz attack.

She leaned out of the window and fired a burst from her own tommy gun at the Fritzes outside. But even as she did so, she knew it was wasted effort. The Fritzes were cunning swine and skilled at their job. They were quickly moving onto 'dead ground' – the entrance had been cleared of her Red Eagles and the Germans were out of her line of fire. '*Boshe moi*', she cursed and told herself she had only minutes to make a decision. Should she leave her girls to fight it out to the death with the attacking Fritzes or should she take whatever force she could collect and escape? For she knew if she dealt with the Fritzes who had slipped by the hotel she might well stop the whole advance – for a little while. In God's name what should she do?

The decision was made for her. Greul, his mind set on that mountain, and almost within grasping distance, was not going to waste any more time and men winkling out the survivors up on the third floor. They would fight to the bitter end in that fatalistic Russian manner of theirs. He could not afford to suffer any further casualties or any further delay. He had already ordered his men to cease fire and merely contain the defenders of the third storey. He would deal with them, as they deserved. If they wouldn't surrender, as he knew the Popov bitches wouldn't, then they would have to die horribly.

The smoke beginning to seep through the cracks in the flooring and drifting up the body-littered shattered stairway to the third floor, told Major Mikailovna all she needed to know. 'Smoke,' she cried in horror, 'they're going to smoke us out . . . *Davoi* . . . *Go!'*

Down below, Greul wiped away the sweat which dripped down his forehead like opaque pearls and laughed in triumph. The relief party threw more and more bits of cheap furniture on the fire which was beginning to blaze in the entrance. Shielding his eyes against the glare, he ordered, 'Keep it going . . . keep it going . . . Five minutes more and the Red bitches will be screaming to surrender . . . But then it will be too late, comrades.' He laughed uproariously. There was no humour in the sound, it was just one of near madness. 'We shall be gone . . .'

Three

'Hypoxia.' The explanation cut into Colonel Sturmer's dulled brain like a sharp knife. As he reached the ledge, two of his best men, waiting to finish the climb, were swaying and shouting at each other furiously. Sturmer knew that they should have been tired and conserving whatever strength they had left after climbing nearly all morning.

Just to make sure that his diagnosis was correct, he looked dully at the altitude meter strapped to his left wrist. The green needle seemed to flicker a lot, even tremble, as if his eyes were losing their ability to focus properly. Dimly he knew why. When he finally managed to get a reading he realized he was correct in his thinking. The altitude meter showed they had reached a height of nearly four thousand, five hundred metres. He, to a lesser extent, and his two soldiers, to a greater one, were suffering from the euphoria that came with hypoxia – the lack of oxygen. '*Grosser Gott*,' he cursed out loud. 'We've got altitude sickness. Shit on the Christmas tree.' For he knew what that meant. The men would have to take a rest and he daren't even think about what that would mean to the timing of the rest of the climb.

'Listen,' he called to the red-faced angry mountaineers. 'You'll find your heads are throbbing . . . as if they're going to burst apart any minute.'

'Yessir,' one of them agreed. He shook his head, as if attempting to clear it like a boxer who had just taken a nasty punch on the jaw might.

Next to him, his comrade added, 'I feel . . . I feel as I'm made of feathers . . . as light as air, sir . . . And I think I'm going to puke . . . lose my cookies at any moment . . .' He swayed alarmingly and avoided falling just in time.

156

Sturmer contained his temper. He knew, as light-headed as he was himself, that it was fatal for a climber to lose control, especially at this height. This was when men made wrong decisions: ones that could lead to sudden death. 'All right, we're stopping now.'

'We'll freeze our eggs off at this height,' someone commented.

Sturmer ignored the comment. They'd keep warm somehow. He explained. 'We're not going any further today. We'll eat and rest, then, with a bit of luck, we'll acclimatize a little better to the air up here by the morrow . . . Come on,' he added reluctantly, 'let's get on with it.'

Mount Elbrus would not be conquered that day.

Back in the mountain village, von Dodenburg looked at his watch for the umpteenth time. He had expected some sort of signal from Colonel Sturmer's mountaineers by now. Von Dodenburg didn't know exactly what that signal would be save that he hoped it would inform him that they were on their way back and he could get them and his own men out and on the road away from this remote region.

He had buried Ox-Jo and Egon hastily among the rocks, though he had felt no shame at having shot the treacherous young driver. Then he had ordered Schulze to give their daily ration to the native women, to cook the cans of old man tinned meat – reputedly made from dead old men from Berlin's workhouses – into a decent meal, which had been accompanied by a thimbleful of the last of their *Korn* for each trooper. He had hoped that a well-cooked spicy meal, plus a sip of the fiery gin would improve the mood of his mixed force. At first it had. But as the second day dragged on and there was no sign of Sturmer returning, he could sense that some of the men, especially the younger ones, even among Wotan's volunteers, were starting to look disgruntled once more.

Von Dodenburg could reason why. During his first venture into Russia when the German autumn offensive against Moscow had begun to stall in the mud and snow, he had fallen victim to a similar mood himself. It was engendered by the endless remoteness of the steppe: the feeling that one could be trapped in this cruel remote country and never escape again. Obviously some of the younger men felt the same, especially as the sun shone over the snow-clad peaks. They reasoned that this was the time to do a bunk while the going was good. For even the rawest greenbeak among them had soon realized that the weather here was changeable, too damnable changeable to be trusted for very long.

Naturally his old hares Schulze and Matz did their best to cheer up the men, especially as von Dodenburg suspected that they had had more than their fair share of the potent alcohol. They talked the language the soldiers understood and which encouraged them more than all the fancy talk about the New Order and the ideals of National Socialism; though, von Dodenburg told himself with a slight grin, as a convinced member of that same New Order he shouldn't even think such things.

'Yes, you greenbeaks.' He heard Schulze saying to a group of his young listeners. 'When I was young and could get an erection like a good diamond cutter even by just thinking of a pair of women's knickers, it wasn't that easy to throw yer leg over some bit of juicy beaver. In them days, long ago, when you lot was still wearing triangular pants – wet at that – yer poor old stubble-hopper had to save up a couple of weeks' pay even to get a sniff of it from an ordinary common-or-garden pavement pounder,' – he meant whore – 'In them days, your average German woman wasn't givin' it away like they do these days, even to a lot of spotty dicks like you lot o' cardboard soldiers.'

But even as he listened, von Dodenburg realized the sexually charged tales of Schulze and Matz weren't really getting through to the anxious young soldiers. Every so often, one of Schulze's listeners would flash a nervous glance up the road towards Mount Elbrus as if he expected a triumphant Colonel Sturmer and his weary climbers to appear over the rise. But Colonel Sturmer stubbornly refused to appear and reluctantly von Dodenburg was forced to accept the fact that the mountain troop officer wouldn't return this night as he had half-promised to do so. They would be forced to spend

158

yet another long, nervy night in the village and he knew from past experience what such nights in Russia did to young jumpy soldiers. He frowned and told himself that if he were still a praying man, which he wasn't – what good National Socialist soldier believed in religion these days? – he'd get out his prayer-mat and get down on his knees.

'So yer see, you greenbeaks.' Schulze was concluding his tale of his youthful sexual deprivation. 'In them days, your poor squaddie had two alternatives – tie it to his frigging leg or go and get hissen a dirty book and have – er – sexual intercourse with the five-fingered widow.' He made an explicit gesture with his clenched right fist. No one laughed.

Sergeant Schulze came over a few minutes later to where von Dodenburg squatted on a rock, deep in thought, and said, 'Miserable bunch of bastards, sir, if you'll forgive my French.'

'I will, Schulze, you big rogue,' von Dodenburg said, half-heartedly returning the big NCO's salute. 'I suppose you understand them?'

Schulze spat into the dirty snow, a look of utter contempt on his tough red face. 'They don't make 'em like they did in the old days when we set off on this glorious crusade to liberate Europe.'

Von Dodenburg knew he should react to Schulze's cynicism, but he simply hadn't the strength to do so. 'All right . . . all right,' he said mildly. 'Save it for your cronies, the old hares.'

'That bunch of greenbeaks over there, sir, are straight off their mother's titty, sir. Willing enough when it comes to parades and flash SS uniforms, but when it comes to the crunch—' He shrugged his shoulders and left the rest of his sentence unsaid.

Von Dodenburg nodded and said, 'I know what you mean. But it's all we got left, Schulze. You've got to understand that – and they're the best we have, too. What they need is a victory – a great victory for German arms and then you'll see, Schulze, they'll become like you and your bunch of hairy-assed old hares, though I pity the greenbeaks if they ever do.' He smiled weakly.

Schulze wasn't convinced. He had known von Dodenburg

159

ever since he had come to Wotan, back before the war, as an eager young lieutenant straight from the SS cadet school at Bad Toelz. In the intervening years they had fought together in battle after battle right across Europe. He felt he could speak frankly to the CO although the latter, he guessed, was still convinced that the New Order had saved Europe from Bolshevism.

'I don't think that even victory will convince them or the rest any more, sir,' Schulze said very quietly to him. 'Even that business with the mountain up there won't. It'll only be a – er – symbol.' He fumbled a little to find the word. 'Something for the press and the Poison Dwarf to get all excited about – just for a couple of days. Then it'll be back to this shitting Russia.' He shook his head, as if he didn't understand the world any longer. 'Russia'll be Germany's downfall.' He paused, his big chest heaving a little in the rarified air with the effort of speaking so much.

Von Dodenburg wasn't offended. He respected Schulze and such old hares. They were the backbone of the Regiment. When the chips were down they'd fight to the death; they had always done so in the past. 'Perhaps, you're right,' he responded slowly, 'and perhaps you're wrong. I hope you are. But one thing is clear, Schulze.' He looked hard at the other man, his light blue eyes hard and steely for an instant.

'And what's that, sir?'

'We've got to continue what we started. You remember the old German saying, 'Went with, caught with, hanged with.*'

'March or croak, like,' Schulze countered with the old Wotan motto.

'Exactly – march or croak.'

Schulze smiled suddenly. 'Well, sir, as Frau Schulze's handsome son doesn't intend to croak just yet, I suppose it's gonna be march.'

Von Dodenburg returned his smile. After Schulze returned to his old running mate, Matz, who was already making plans for the troopers' evening meal in the hope that he might

*From a medieval German saying, '*Mitgegangan, mitgefangen, mitgehangen.*' Transl.

160

get another nip of that delectable *Korn*, von Dodenburg's smile vanished.

He remembered, as if in an almost forgotten dream, how it had all started: the pride, the brassy bombast, the black-clad elite, giants all, goose-stepping down the *Unter den Linden* in perfect formation, ten abreast, the click of a thousand helmeted heads turning in the direction of the Führer as he saluted them. Back then there had seemed no stopping them. How could anyone stop these blond giants with that frightening SS on their helmets and the silver cross-and-bones on their lapels, symbolizing their dedication to death for the holy cause of National Socialism. First the sub-humans and inferior races – the Poles, the Belgians, the Dutch had run before them. The French had followed. Even the English had fled from a fighting force, the like of which no one had seen in the Old Continent since the time of the all-conquering Roman legions.

It had been the same in Greece, Yugoslavia, the rest of the Balkans. Victory after victory. They were unstoppable. The natives had welcomed them not as conquerors, but as liberators. At first it had been the same in Russia. They had been pelted with flowers, given the traditional bread and salt, the symbol of welcome. After all they were freeing the hard-pressed peasants from their bolshevik oppressors. Men, who should have been their enemies, had flocked to the blood-red banner of National Socialism by their hundreds, thousands, hundreds of thousands. Dutch, Belgian, French and half a dozen races in the East had volunteered for the German Armed Forces. Some said there were even English in the ranks of the Armed SS these days. What had seemed a great European Liberation Army had fought against Russia. But in that country the Great Dream had ended . . .

Kuno von Dodenburg stopped. Behind him a column of thick black smoke, sinister and threatening, was beginning to ascend into the darkening afternoon sky. With sinking heart, the young arrogant officer knew that it could only be a signal. Of what? . . . Disaster!

161

Four

Major Mikailovna removed her snow-clogged goggles, wiped them and stared back at the burning hotel. There seemed to be about twenty Red Eagles left spread out in the snow in a long line, outlined in a stark black against the pure whiteness and the cherry red flames licking up at the building they had abandoned some thirty minutes before.

She had known that she was taking a great risk by setting light to the place with her own force seemingly trapped in the upper floor. Happily the sudden snowstorm had given her the cover she had needed to get them out while the Fritzes below had been occupied by the surprising blaze. Naturally the Fritzes, as always, had damn well recovered swiftly and the shooting had commenced. Her Eagles caught on the outside, easy targets against the snow, had fallen everywhere. She was relieved to be well away from the burning building with twenty of her Eagles still on their feet; the Major reasoned they'd be sufficient to stop the Fritzes up ahead on the mountain. She justified the death of so many of her brave girls to herself: they sacrificed themselves for Mother Russia and the great patriotic war

She gave the signal for her Eagles to continue their advance. They responded immediately. They, too, wanted revenge for their dead comrades and to do their utmost for their country. Ignoring the flames behind them, they plunged forwards through the sudden snow, dwarfed into insignificance by the mighty peaks to left and right.

The Major knew that they were not as fit and as experienced as she was, although some of them were almost half her age – they needed more rest than she did – but she dare not let them rest. Time was of the essence. She had to stop the Fritzes. How, she did not know exactly yet, but stop them she would.

So they toiled forward, their bodies racked with pain, their breath coming in harsh gasps. Frozen snow lashed their crimson faces. It ripped their skins like cuts from a sharp knife. Still they didn't bleed; the icy wind froze any blood that might have seeped through. On and on they plodded. They were beginning to climb upwards. The slope, as yet, was not steep, at least for them. Still, each step seemed to take a major effort of willpower. An immense weight appeared to be attached to each foot and their fingers, searching frantically for handholds to support them, felt like great clumsy sausages. Still, the Major brooked no slacking or stopping. '*Davoi . . . davoi,*' she chanted above the howl of the wind like some religious litany. '*Davoi,* my brave eagles . . .'

The snow had covered the tracks of the Fritzes who had started the climb well ahead of the Eagles, heading straight for the mountain. The Major was not overly concerned yet. Just behind her was a member of her Eagles whom the rest called the Siberian Sniffer Dog. She was an oversized, tubby girl in her early twenties. The Major had been informed the girl came from Siberian, though her flat, high-cheeked, somewhat greasy face made the Major think she came from further north, perhaps from one of Russia's outposts on the Baring Sea. Not that she could confirm this, for the Siberian Sniffer Dog was monosyllabic in her very limited Russian. Besides when on patrol, she went on ahead, urging the others forward with her strange chant, 'I smell Fritz . . . come you quick.'

It was true. Even with the Fritzes' tracks obscured by fresh snowfall, she was straining at the leash to take over the point, uttering her weird chant, 'I smell Fritz . . . come you quick.'

Major Mikailovna reasoned confidently that the Siberian Sniffer Dog – dressed in a thick coat, covered in snow, looking rather like a chubby little dog – would find the enemy.

They advanced. On and on. Step by step. Lurching, stumbling, shaking, choked at times by terrible winds which swept relentlessly across the high peaks, sometimes almost knocking the Red Eagles off their feet. Trained as they were for such heights, even they began now to feel and suffer the effects of the rarified atmosphere. Their ears popped. One after another, they were struck by severe headaches. It took them a super-human effort almost to draw a single breath. Every so often an Eagle cried out or moaned piteously, raising one arm as if appealing to some God to put an end to her misery. Today God was looking the other way.

Once a great howling wind tore at their bodies as they eased their way along a treacherous narrow shelf of rock, made worse by the wet snow. For what seemed an age they clung to each other like frightened children, who feared the wind might fling them to their deaths far below. The wind passed and they floundered on, animated now by the Siberian Sniffer Dog's weird chant, 'I smell Fritz . . . come you quick!'

Quick they were not but Major Mikailovna saw with pride that not one of her Red Eagles had fallen out of formation. They were still moving forward, even the weakest of her girls.

Time passed leadenly. Then the wind started to die – and with it the snowstorm. It seemed ages before the Red Eagles noticed. Chins sunk on their snow-covered chests, they continued as before, struggling along the face of the great mountain, concentrating totally on each new step. With infinite weariness the Major raised her head and finally realized, as she stared at the dying flakes in apparent bewilderment, that the storm was over.

They paused and gasped like someone who had just run a great race. A hush descended on the ascent, broken no longer by that terrible howling wind, but by their harsh breathing. What did it mean? they seemed to ask. Slowly they began to consume the air that the wind had torn from their oxygen-starved lungs. They breathed more easily. Their headaches and the feverish trembling of their hands started to abate. They became almost normal human beings once more, who could see and hear and reason logically.

Suddenly they were alert to that strange cry of the Siberian Sniffer Dog. This time it was not that she had scented the Fritzes. This time she cried, 'Look, comrades . . . *Fritzes*!'

It had been a terrible night for Sturmer and his little team. Somehow despite the terrible storm, they had managed to get their little primus stoves to work. The stoves were starved of oxygen just as they were. The tired blue, wildly flickering flames had seemed to take an age to boil the drink that Sturmer, the expert, knew the sick among his men needed urgently. Those suffering from altitude sickness had finally been able to consume the strong mixture of coffee, condensed milk and as much sugar as they could find; to give them new energy that they vitally needed.

It had worked. Sturmer had waited patiently till everyone else had had half a canteen of the powerful mix before he had taken his share. Almost immediately he had sensed the oxygen beginning to flow through his body again. The weariness fled his limbs. Energy surged through his lean body and once more he faced up to the challenge. One of his troopers, leaning against his rucksack and chewing on iron-hard salami, cried, '*Teufel und Titten* . . . I could conquer the world.'

Sturmer had grinned happily at the sudden cry, approving the man's sentiments, though for the life of him, he couldn't imagine what the 'Devil and Tits' had to do with it. He did not waste time querying the relationship. The snowstorm had finished and the last of the clouds had vanished. A cold sun had risen casting its cold rosy-hued light over the final slope ahead. The snow particles glittered in its light like a myriad of tiny diamonds. It was like a snow-scene on a *kitsch* pre-war Christmas card, snow and sun. All that was lacking was a sleigh and a snow-heavy fir tree complete with burning candles. Sturmer's heart leapt joyfully at the scene, and more so when he saw what lay above the slope. There were the twin peaks of Mount Elbrus looking down upon them in remote mysterious silence. For a moment he was entranced. He had never seen the peaks so close and their strange alien remoteness was beautiful. He felt as stirred as he had done as a small child and he had gazed from his frozen bedroom window to exclaim in wonder to the world, '*It's snowed . . . Daddy, it's snowed!*'

Sturmer could contain himself no longer. They had almost

165

done it. 'All right, you lazy louts,' he cried, 'do you want to rest here for ever? Are you with me?' Carried away by their CO's enthusiasm, they cried as one, their young voices bright and clear, 'Lead on, sir . . . we're with you.'

Greul was also carried away by an almost unreasoning enthusiasm. Later when the Poison Dwarf personally asked in Berlin on the eve of the great parade, why Greul had been so enthusiastic in the light of the privations that he and his men were suffering that day, he had been unable to reply at first. What emotions had been going through his head as they had made their way forward in the wake of the Soviet bitches who had escaped under the cover of the fire and the great snowstorm which had followed. In the end, Greul had been forced to recourse to the kind of explanation which the undersized, club-footed Minister of Propaganda and Public Enlightenment would like. '*Herr* Minister,' he had declared, towering above the cynical little man with his dark knowing eyes, 'I did it for the Fatherland. I and my brave fellows knew that no sacrifice could be too great for the future of our National Socialist cause.'

The Poison Dwarf had liked that. 'Well said,' he had replied. Still he had not been quite able to shake off his suspicious cynicism, adding, 'Naturally you didn't think of the great honours that the Führer would bestow on you.' He had indicated towards the Knight's Cross of the Iron Cross dangling from Greul's throat.

'*Nein, Herr Minister,*' he had replied stiffly. Of course, those honours had animated him.

Greul's promises to his reluctant men had kept them going, after he had abandoned two of their seriously wounded comrades in the smouldering lower storey of the hotel.

'There'll be a week's leave for every one of you. I promise you . . . And the Iron Cross to make your families proud of you . . . I personally will ensure that you have the services of the ladies of the night at my own expense once we reach the Reich once more . . .'

Lie after lie, just to keep these reluctant heroes, who had no feeling for the greatness of the New Order, but were really

166

ordinary men, who had no vision higher than their sexual organs and their guts.

The lies had kept them going. As the snowstorm abated, in the clear air of the mountains, so rarified that if he had wished he could have looked for kilometres, Greul saw the two groups of stark black, stick figures, outlined against the white glare of the snowfield, separated by only a couple of hundred metres toiling up the mountain that he had come so far to climb – and he knew now that *he* was the one who was going to conquer it.

Neither party was unaware of each other. But they did not know about him and his group, he was sure of that. Both groups had their gazes fixed on the ultimate objective – the peak.

Greul was right. Sturmer was concentrating solely on the peak and the fifty-five degree angle of the slope which led up to it. Under normal circumstances as an experienced mountaineer, the steepness would not have worried him. But this slope was covered by a thin film of snow and below that lay pure ice. Time and time again, he and his men slipped and fell on the stuff, cursing heartily as they did so for it was wearing them out and at that alttitude making their pulses race at an alarming rate. Soon, if this went on, Sturmer knew they would start suffering seriously from the lack of oxygen and the dreaded altitude fever. Once that set in, they'd never make the peak and commence the descent again today; and with their energy sapped, the intense night cold and the lack of supplies, that might well mean they'd die on Mount Elbrus.

He paused for a few moments. Glancing at his watch and then at the altitude meter on his other wrist he announced, 'Plenty of time still.' Then added, 'We're almost there. Nearly seven thousand metres.' It was a lie. But a necessary one.

'Then we've got the worse part behind us, sir,' one of his men gasped.

'Yes, and the ice slope is coming to an end. It'll be roses all the way now. Another hundred and two metres, my fine fellows, and you'll all be heroes when we get back home. Why, girls'll be asking for autographs and in Berlin they'll be selling postcard pictures of yer ugly mugs, just like they do of Hans Albers* and that lot of film stars.'

'*Auf gehts*,' someone yelled with real enthusiasm.

'*Auf gehts*,' the cry was taken up by the others and once more they commenced that terrible climb, each man animated by his own thoughts of the splendid future the CO had promised them: girls and drink and medals. The dreams of young näive men who did not realize that in reality they were doomed to die an early and probably violent death.

Half an hour later, with the western peak so clearly defined in the sun and the air so thick it seemed they could almost touch it, Sturmer stopped his exhausted men and, with frozen fingers that felt like thick clumsy sausages, he pulled out two bars of chocolate that he had saved for the occasion. He followed that by groping in his rucksack and pulling out the carefully folded banner of the New Order. Bit by bit almost pedantically he broke up the plain chocolate, which contained the only stimulants left to them, dextrose sugar and pervitin, the drug. One by one, his men stumbled forward at his command and accepted their pathetic bit of chocolate. Sturmer told them, 'Chew it carefully. Savour every morsel. You need the energy. For this is it, comrades.'

They were too greedy for the sugar to understand what the CO meant. And finally, after they had swallowed their chocolate, licking their cracked lips, they moved.

The straggle of weary mountaineers reached that long sought after western peak of Mount Elbrus in, what the handful of survivors remembered long afterwards as being, a completely undramatic manner. One moment they were still totally concentrated on savouring that little bit of chocolate. 'God, how we licked our chops then, as if that bit o' sugar was a great big plateful of sauerkraut and pig knuckle and there it was . . . *Himmelherrje*, you could have knocked me over with a frigging feather.'

As they came abruptly to a slight rise, there was a stretch of wind-flattened snow, virginal and perfectly smooth. It led to a gentle cone. Beyond there was a sky of intense blue,

*Well-known comic movie star of the time.

168

revealing the Caucasian plain and the road to Asia beyond. It must have been for those dead tired mountaineers, if they had known about such matters, like Cortez of the Spanish *conquistadoree* seeing the Pacific for the first time, the first European to do so back in the sixteen century.

They staggered to a stop. Sturmer actually sat down suddenly in the snow, as if some unseen hand had pushed him over. He swallowed hard and for the first time since they had started that terrible ascent, he didn't have to bellow. In a small voice, full of wonder, he said, 'Comrade . . . comrades, we've reached the summit.' He broke off, too overcome with emotion to say any more.

A couple of metres away, one of the older mountaineers said incredulously. 'But is this it, sir? You mean, that's all?' He pointed wearily at the gentle white cone in front of them.

Numbly Sturmer nodded.

The man next to the older Bavarian added, 'Well, I'll piss in my dice-beaker. All that frigging carry-on . . . losing the lads and everything.' He pushed back his peaked cap and scratched his cropped head in bewilderment. 'Was it worth it, sir?'

Sturmer looked at the man's sun-tanned emaciated face and could understand the simple soldier's bewilderment. In another age, he would have jumped on the fellow, shouted at him that they had achieved something the like of which few men would achieve in their whole lives. But not now. As much as he felt an inner glow, an almost sexual frisson, at what they had just done, he knew, too, that all he had achieved in this year of 1942 was to flatter the ego and power dreams of some National Socialist fanatic. What they had just done would be used for a purpose that he hated – propaganda for that '1,000 Year Reich', that Hitler dreamed about. But he must not tell his loyal soldiers that. He had to convince them that all their hardships, their effort, the sacrifice of their dead comrades had to be for something.

He made the effort and pulled himself to his feet a little wearily. He stretched his arm out to encompass the plain beyond the peak. 'Somewhere out there, comrades, there is

169

Asia . . . the Caspian Sea, Persia, Afghanistan, ours for the taking. If we capture those territories and link up with our Japanese allies, already fighting in India, we Germans will create an empire greater than the one carved out by the force of his arms, than Alexander the Great himself. Why, comrades,' he grew expansive, for he felt the men were still staring at him in bewilderment, perhaps wondering who in three devils' name, this Alexander the Great was. 'Do you realize that we are over four thousand kilometres from Munich. Isn't that something?'

Despite his rhetoric, his men weren't impressed. The one who had spoken first spat on the ground, not even looking at Asia beyond, saying, 'Forgive me, sir, but I'd take Munich any day . . . a litre of good Lowenbrau suds, a plate of fried taties and a big whore with plenty of wood in front of the door and I, for one, would be a happy man!'

'*Jawohl*,' the others growled in agreement.

Sturmer gave in. He forced a grin. 'All right, comrades, have it your way. Let's get on with the flag raising ceremony so that I can take a photo of it for those rear echelon stallions back in Berlin in their fancy uniforms.' He fumbled in his rucksack for the flag that had accompanied them over this long journey. 'Then you can get back to Munich, your suds and fodder.' His grin broadened. 'And the whores with plenty of wood before the door.'

Greul was narrowing the gap between his own group and the Russian bitches rapidly, but the Red Eagles, under Major Mikailovna was still not aware of the second group of Fritzes to her rear. Her gaze was fixed intently on the little group of Germans grouped around a makeshift flag-pole on the peak. Indeed, carried away by her hatred of these invaders who had conquered the highest mountain in the Caucasus, she had still not realized that she and her Red Eagles were within fifty or sixty metres of doing the same thing. Hate blinded her to everything but the overwhelming necessity of stopping the Fritzes.

Greul's mind raced as he closed the gap on the unsuspecting Russians. It was clear that soon the Popovs would

170

engage Sturmer on the height in a fire fight. Naturally the Red bitches didn't know that he and his men were so close on their heels and that, to all intents and purposes, they were trapped between two parties of German troops. Indeed Greul knew expert marksmen, such as his men, could deal with the Popovs, so clearly outlined against the snow, even at this range. But what would be in that for him? All it would mean, if he dealt with the Russians, was that Sturmer, an officer he had come not only to envy, but to also hate, would gain the kudos of being the man who had conquered Mount Elbrus. It would be Colonel Sturmer who would be promoted, awarded the medals, be feted by the party *prominenz* and probably be received by the Führer himself. But did Sturmer deserve it? Wasn't he the officer who derided the achievements of National Socialism and the New Order? Why should he, a virtual anti-Nazi, come to represent all that was good, even holy: everything that he, Siegfried Greul, had believed in since he had been a teenager in the short black pants of the Führer's Hitler Youth? How could he replace the unbeliever who in a few moments would plant the holy flag of the New Order on that peak?

As the little column hurried ever faster to catch up with the Popovs, Greul's rage grew and grew in intensity. He saw that the bitch at the head of the Popovs was beginning to unsling a strange-looking, overlong rifle from her back. For a moment he was puzzled. Then he caught the momentary glint of a lens in the sunrays. It was a sniper's rifle, one of those World War One rifles that the Russian snipers, the swine, always used to deadly effect.

The Popovs closed in as Sturmer and his men grouped round their makeshift flag pole. The Russian was wrapping the leather strap around her left arm to give the weapon more stability when she fired. But at whom was she going to do so? In a flash it came to him. The bitch was going to shoot Sturmer, the man with the flag, which he was shaking out before attaching it to the pole. He opened his mouth to cry a warning but caught himself in time. Why should he warn Sturmer? They were both Germans admittedly, but in their thinking and attitude they were as far away from one

171

another, as the earth is from the sun. Slowly, almost audibly, he closed his mouth and let what had to happen, happen . . .

The Major squinted along the sight. A bronzed weary-looking face slid silently into the gleaming circle of calibrated glass. Delicately she adjusted the focus, as if she were a well-trained high school student adjusting the needle of her school sewing machine. The face of the Fritz she would kill leapt into the circle of glass clearly. Now she could see every detail of him. The Fritz looked every bit a soldier. Yet there was something understanding, even kind about the face, it was not the look she associated with the brutal conquerors who had ravished Mother Russia. She wondered for a second what type of man this Fritz was, whom she was about to kill. She saw how he moved, as if in slow motion as he raised the crooked cross banner of the invaders. He moved in a manner she could not help, but think reverently, not as victor, a conqueror of people and mountains, but almost as a lover.

Her knuckles whitened. She took first pressure, feeling the hard surety of the brass rifle butt tucked into her right shoulder. On the little peak, the man she would kill had raised his hand to his peaked cap in salute. She pressed her trigger. A sharp crack. A smell of burned gunpowder. The butt slapped back into her shoulder. Nothing seemed to happen at first. For one frightening instant she thought she had missed. She hadn't. Slowly, infinitely slowly, the big Fritz's legs started to crumple. His cap slid comically to one side of his abruptly red-stained head. Without warning, he pitched face-forward into the snow.

'Hurrah!' the Siberian Sniffer Dog yelled wildly, breaking the spell. 'You kill, Comrade Major . . .' The cry of triumph turned into a scream of absolute agony, as Greul's first burst seemed to saw the dumpy little woman in half, her blood spurting in every direction, splashing up and across Major Mikailovna's face, momentarily blinding her.

'The Fritzes . . . The Fritzes, they're behind us,' several of the Red Eagles shouted in sudden alarm. Too late. They didn't stand a chance. At that range Greul's men couldn't miss. They fired into the women mercilessly, carried away by their unreasoning blood-lust.

The Major was the first to realize that they had walked into a trap. She dropped the rifle and darted forward to the edge of the little plateau. She'd throw herself over the side and take the chance that she'd break her fall before it was too late. But it wasn't to be. As she started, with the German bullets whipping up the snow in frenzied little spurts around her flying feet, her Eagles scattering, only to be mown down themselves mercilessly, the ground gave way beneath her.

She screamed. She slithered down faster and faster. The scream trailed behind her, as the Germans completed their deadly work. All the troopers were petrified by that awful, long drawn out scream which sent shivers down their backs. On and on it went, as the slither became a fatal roll, getting further and further away down the mountain until the snow fell away altogether and Major Mikailovna, the founder of the Red Eagles, sailed out into space, death waiting for her far below.

There was nothing left but a loud echoing silence which seemed to go on and on for ever. Above, that cruel crooked cross that had brought terror and death to the whole of the Old Continent hung limp on its make-shift post, dead itself. The mountain had beaten them all.

Envoi

It was Führer weather. Over Berlin, the sky was a perfect blue. The sun shone in a bright yellow ball. But its heat, which would have been oppressive this August day, 1942, was eased by the faint gentle wind from the east. Tiny dust devils rose in its path. They settled on the highly polished, elegant riding boots of the generals and whipped up the fashionable hems of their womenfolk's Paris dresses. They didn't seem to notice. After all, what was a little dust on a day of celebration like this? Besides their maids and batmen would take care of the dust in due course. What else were servants for?

Naturally all of Berlin was present. Everyone of any importance wanted to see and be seen. Of course, they wanted to welcome the returning heroes and reflect in their glory, but it was the social scene that had really brought them here, away from their offices and ministries. Afterwards at the receptions and the new-fangled champagne and cocktail parties they would have a good gossip about Frau Baronin X and her new lover and Herr General der Infanterie Y and that absurdly young secretary he was sleeping with while his dowdy middle-aged wife in her size forty bloomers lanquished on their new estate in East Prussia. Shortly after the heroes would be forgotten but today they must honour them, such brave boys, as they claimed they were.

They waited; the brown uniformed paunchy *Gauleiters* in their chocolate brown party uniform; the leaders of the Party's youth organizations, the League of German Maidens, Beauty and Belief, the Young Folk – all middle-aged men and women, looking a little absurd in their brief shorts and too short skirts; the ambassadors of Germany's allies, Bulgaria,

177

Slovakia, Romania, Finland. Even Baron Oshima, bespectacled and bulging yellow teeth, the Japanese envoy to the Reich was there; the Führer had personally declared him an honorary Aryan.

Facing them in the middle of the square was a battalion of the nineth Berlin Guards, every one of them a giant. They looked immaculate in their pressed clean uniforms and gleaming jackboots. How different they looked to the company of Wotan troopers in their shabby patched uniforms. For the regiment had been brought back hastily from the front for this special occasion. Schulze and Matz, the two rogues, were already eyeing up the *prominenz* in the roped-off area to the front, reserved for the honoured guests of the Minister of Propaganda and Public Enlightenment. No fools, they weren't going to waste their precious time in this paradise on common-or-garden pavement punters who, as they expressed it, 'won't give yer poor old stubble hopper a quick feel of titty without payment'. They were after high-born ladies and eager young party virgins, only too ready to sacrifice themselves to evil-minded, randy old hares like them. 'And ones that will buy us plenty o' good suds as well,' Matz reminded Schulze hastily. 'I'm not gonna go back to the front sober, old house. You can rely on that . . .'

For the time being the lecherous duo had to play their part in the ceremony in payment for the delights to come. '*Still gestanden,*' the loud voice of the Guards Battalion commander cut into their sexual reverie. The guard clicked to attention, raising a cloud of dust as their steel-shod boots smashed to the ground. To their rear the garrison band clashed into the brassy blare of the *Deutschlandlied*, the national anthem, their instruments flashing silver and gold in the bright sunshine.

As the last verse of the national anthem died away, the Guards Commander shrieked, 'Guard Battalion – present arms.' Eight hundred pairs of gloved hands completed the intricate drill movement Standing rigidly to attention, gaze set on some distant horizon, their hard hands slapped the well-oiled butts of their rifles and then they were standing with their weapons at the present. Again the band struck up.

178

It was the slow march of the *Gebirgsjager*, those who had survived the Caucasus were joined by scores of new recruits. Immediately the *prominenz* started to clap, the generals saluted, the diplomats took off their top hats and the ordinary crowd cheered, while Goebbels' cameramen swung their cameras back and forth recording the march-by of the 'Victors of Mount Elbrus', as they were now being called.

In front came the newly promoted Colonel Greul, the Knight's Cross of the Iron Cross springing back and forth at his throat, as he goose-stepped at the head of his mountaineers, his every movement expressing his pride at this moment of public acclaim, telling himself as he led his battalion that he must be the very epitome of the National Socialist New Order.

Then, with startling suddenness the band ceased playing. The only sound left was the harsh stamp on the asphalt of the mountaineers' boots. The silence from the crowds was shattered a moment later when a well-known and well-loved figure came on to the podium next to Goebbels. Surrounded and dwarfed by his giant, black-clad SS adjutant, it was the Führer himself. Immediately the crowd broke into frenzied cheering, working men throwing off their caps in their excitement, women breaking down and sobbing almost hysterically, as if they had just lost a loved one. Some even had sudden dark damp patches on their floral frocks, as if they might well have wet themselves in the frenzy.

Out of the side of his mouth, Schulze whispered – for even he feared the Gestapo, who lurked everywhere – to Matz. 'Holy cow, even *he* doesn't piss through his ribs. Why are they going on like this?'

Matz didn't vouchsafe an answer. It was too dangerous. Instead he hissed back, 'Shut your frigging big trap, you idiot . . . you don't want us landing up in the camps, being turned into soap to clean the unwashed masses.'

Schulze, for once, headed his running mate's warning; his mouth closed like a metal snare being sprung.

Von Dodenburg, watching with the other officers of Wotan, scratched himself unconsciously, for like all the Wotan men he was lousy with lice and hadn't had time to be de-loused

179

in the journey back to the Reich from the front in Russia. He looked at Greul standing proudly in front of the Führer, sword momentarily raised to his face in salute. What overwhelming pride seemed to come from the mountain colonel. He had conquered the mountain for the sake of his own vanity – and the Führer's ambitious plans. Greul gave no sign that he remembered the men, good and bad, who had sacrificed themselves so that he could realize that objective, which had become merely an instrument of the Poison Dwarf's propaganda.

For a moment or two, von Dodenburg thought of the dead Colonel Sturmer and his dream. *He* had never wanted to *conquer* mountains. His aims were loftier, not concerned with national pride and the furtherance of a political creed. Perhaps Colonel Sturmer, he reasoned, was better off dead.

'Silly fool,' a harsh voice rasped at the back of his mind warningly, 'what kind of talk is that from an officer of the Führer's own SS. Don't even think such treacherous, dangerous thoughts. Clear?'

It was clear. Von Dodenburg dismissed the thought from his mind. Colonel Sturmer would be consigned from now on to an obscure footnote in the history of World War Two, as so many others in von Dodenburg's wartime career had been. All that effort and despair, the heroism, the self-sacrifice, the triumphs and tragedies had to be forgotten till the war reached the end, whenever that might be.

Von Dodenburg, like so many other sensitive young men of his class and time, watched the rest of the parade, wondering idly if he might get permission from the Vulture to go over to the famed Hotel Adlon, take a bath, change into a more respectable uniform, complete with his medals and pick up some high-born lady with patriotic principles who would bed him on the only night the regiment would spend in the capital before it returned to the harsh, brutal reality of the front.

Schulze and Matz needed neither bath, nor a change of uniform. What they needed, as a drunken Schulze confirmed, rather too loudly, to an equally drunken Matz, was 'a slice of the two-legged beast, you Bavarian barnshitter.'

Matz had agreed, but being the more cautious of the two, he objected, 'But who'd take us on, Schulzi? In this frigging uniform, with the frigging lice nibbling away at my frigging pubic hair. Not even a broken-down old pavement pounder on her last legs with a nasty case of clap would want us, even if we had anything to pay her with – which we ain't.'

Schulze laughed boldly, showing the gap in his front teeth which a too bold Popov infantryman had caused with a blow from his rifle butt – the Popov had not survived to admire his handiwork. '*Pavement pounder*, you little asparagus Tarzan,' he exclaimed. 'Haven't you got all yer cups in yer cupboard, *Kumpel*. The elite of the SS *don't* pay for it. If anything, arse-with-ears, they'll pay *us.*'

'Who?'

'The frigging upper-classes, that's who,' his running mate announced triumphantly. 'They know that nothing's too good for the boys in the service. Get your dirty digit outa yer dirty orifice and follow yours truly.'

Schulze had been right. The guard on the entrance of the grand Hotel Adlon had whipped them up a tremendous salute as they had staggered up, barging several high-ranking officers out of the way whispering with a knowing wink as they passed, 'Good hunting, lads.'

In the lift, heavy with expensive perfume, a general's wife had fumbled with Matz's flies, cradling his penis in her delicate hands, as if it were a very precious object, cooing, 'Oh you poor boy, how you must have suffered at the front.' Even the large louse which sprang across and immediately buried itself deep into her enormous bosoms didn't cause her to cease her fondling.

As the lift opened, Matz and Schulze, intent on younger female flesh, vanished into the elegant throng, eyes narrowed like those of a hunter seeking his prey. Matz was still limping slightly as a result of the general's wife's energetic fondling. 'Great crap on the Christmas tree,' Schulze breathed, grabbing a bottle of champagne from a nearby table and taking a great swig of it straight from the neck, 'it's a soldier's dream.'

'Yer right there, Schulze,' Matz agreed, 'If I ever go to frigging heaven – I hope it's gonna be like this.'

Schulze nodded, but said nothing. He was too busy taking in the glittering elegant scene. From all sides came sounds of the rich and prosperous: the tinkle of medals, the clink of tall glasses of champagne being touched in toast; the flashlights exploding blindingly – and everywhere tall elegant women moving in their slow langorous fashion, in the arrogant manner of the rich, who knew no hurry and knew, too, that they could buy even time with their money.

Finally Schulze spoke. 'I once read somewhere—'

'I didn't know you could,' Matz interjected, eyeing up a general's wife, who seemed to be wearing nothing but a negligee trimmed with ostrich feathers. She was bending too low over a table of canapés, revealing white breasts like soft melons.

'Shut up. As I said, I once read that Blucher* said when he reached London after the Battle of Waterloo, this'd be a good place to plunder.'

'So?' Matz queried, licking his dry lips as he prepared to assault those beautiful dangling tits.

'So. This place'd be a good place to plunder, too. It's ripe for the plucking.'

'You said plucking?'

Schulze ignored the comment. 'Let's plunder,' he growled, face fierce and red, as if he were going into the assault on some disputed battlefield barricade.

'Let's plunder.' Matz agreed heartily. Moments later he was hanging on to the arm of the general's wife – with the breasts like melons – leading her up the elegant stairs to the bedrooms beyond. She whispered in his dirty ear, 'Come with me, my little mountain man, I promise you I shall show you some peaks that you've never seen before.' She stroked his dirty face with a pale hand, tipped with red nails as if they were dripping blood.

At the head of the stairs, von Dodenburg, still unchanged and unbathed, feeling like a ragged tramp, watched with a

* Wellington's ally, the Prussian field marshal.

182

smile. The two rogues deserved all they could get. This elegant make-believe, self-important world bore no resemblance to that of the front. Despite the apparent elegance and sophistication it was, in reality, cheap and tawdry; as far from the brutal violent life of men like Schulze and Matz as the moon was from the earth.

Suddenly he was reminded of Colonel Sturmer once more. Perhaps he had been right after all? Then he forgot Matz, Schulze, Colonel Sturmer and all the rest of them. What did they – and he – matter? There was only one solution. He grabbed a passing waiter and threw a fifty mark note on the silver platter he was bearing. 'A bottle of schnapps,' he ordered, 'and a whore, if you can find me one. There'll be another fifty marks in it, if you can.'

The waiter didn't bat an eyelid. 'Yes sir,' he said, in the urbane fashion of high-class waiters in top hotels all over the world. 'Blonde, brunette, any particular type, sir?'

Von Dodenburg was tempted to say a crude word. He desisted. Instead he said, 'One that can bring oblivion, if you know what I mean, Herr Ober.'

'Certainly, sir. As you wish, sir . . . One that can bring oblivion.'